A ROSE RIDGE CHRISTMAS
A STONE RIDER NOVELLA

ASHLEY MUÑOZ

Copyright © 2024 by Zetalife LLC
& Ashley Munoz
ISBN:9798300835712
All rights reserved.
No part of this book may be reproduced in any form or by any electronic or mechanical means, including information storage and retrieval systems, without written permission from the author, except for the use of brief quotations in a book review.
No AI training of any kind is permitted.

Cover Design: Wildheart Graphics
Beta/ Content Editing: Memos in the Margins
Editing: Rebecca's Fairest Reviews
Proofing: Tiffany Hernandez

❦ Created with Vellum

AN IMPORTANT NOTE

This timeline is ten years after Silas and Natty's story finishes. However, it's important to note that the next book coming will go back in time, to shortly after Where We Ended stopped.

This novella is more of a glimpse, with a bunch of subtle foreshadowing. It is fast-paced and is supposed to feel like you were dropped into a scene in their lives while just standing in the shadows, watching it all unfold from various perspectives.

It won't make sense unless you've read the full series, AND it would be helpful to have read the bonus content from books 3 and 4. Which can be found on my website under bonus content.* www.ashleymunozbooks.com/bonuscontent

Stone Rider
Family Trees

Callie & Wes Ryan

FORD (AGE 10)   ELLIE (AGE 7)

Killian & Laura Quinn

ROYCE (AGE 9)   TARYN (AGE 7)

Penelope & Jameson King

NOVA (AGE 7)   CONNOR (AGE 10)

Silas & Natty Silva

ROOK (AGE 9)   RYLE (AGE 6)

ONE
CALLIE

Snow was rarely guaranteed in Rose Ridge, especially during the month of December.

When it did stick to the ground, or cause enough of a reaction, the entire town seemed to collectively smile. Everyone appeared happier, as if there wasn't a single problem in the world. We were in a snow globe, and while we all knew our proverbial happiness was made of glass and could shatter…no one seemed to care.

"How will they decide who the winner is?" Ellie, my seven-year-old, asked while pulling open the door to The Drip.

The smell of freshly baked cupcakes curled around us, the warmth of the room immediately pulling us in. Ellie was already stripping off layers as she walked toward the glass case of goodies. It was what she always did, and the second she'd arrive, her nose would press firmly against the surface, creating a mark that Natty never complained about. Even if her baristas always gave my little girl the side-eye.

Ford let out an irritated sigh. "This is baby stuff, Mom. Why can't I head over to Connor's and play that new game he got?"

Ten years old, and he was already showing signs of being a moody teenager.

"Connor is coming here, so you'll both be joining our annual Christmas cookie exchange whether you want to or not." I said, trying to push off the sadness over how grown up the two boys were. A decade had flown by in a blink, and I was still trying to play catch up.

Ford walked past his sister, heading toward the back of the café.

A few patrons were seated around the room, but Natty's staff was behind the counter, assisting everyone. I smiled at Shaylee, one of the baristas that had just started working here after I talked to Natty on her behalf. Her boyfriend was a tattoo artist over at Dead Roses.

"You guys have fun!" Shaylee called as I walked past her to the kitchen; Ellie was quick to run alongside me as we both pushed in through the kitchen doors.

I smiled as Natty stood against a long counter, her golden hair wavy from wearing braids. She wore a black apron with faded lettering across the chest. It looked like the same one Silas had gifted her, her one and only property patch that she wore since her husband left the club behind. We all assumed he'd maybe one day patch back in with the Stone Riders, but he never did. He rode with them when and if they needed him, but if he did, he wore the patch the guys gave him.

The one they meant as a joke, but Silas still wore it. It was his property patch that said he belonged to Natty.

"You guys made it!" Natty spotted us and set down her lump of cookie dough.

My gaze dropped to the two raven haired boys at her side, who were covered in flour and freckles. Silas and Natty had two beautiful sons, and somehow, they both turned out to be little miniature versions of Silas. Black hair, light blue eyes, so bright, they looked as if they weren't of this world. Their oldest, Rook, who was closer to Ford's age, had just turned nine and looked the most like Silas out of the two. He had his father's nose and mouth. Their youngest, Ryle, was only six years old, but he was more like Natty. He still had dark hair and light blue eyes, but he had her mouth, nose and cheeks. He also had her temperament, loving nature and staring at the clouds.

"Hi Rook." Ellie waved like she always did. She was better friends with Ryle, but Rook always seemed to make her nervous and her cute little cheeks would flush pink.

Rook glanced up quickly and muttered a quick hello before returning to the cookie dough in front of him.

I unloaded my coat and purse on the table near the door and watched as Natty began helping my kids into aprons.

"This says my name on it." Ellie traced her little finger over the white lettering on her pink apron.

Ford lifted the black one up over his head and darted his gaze down to the letters on his.

Natty beamed, while returning to her station. She sprinkled flour on a new section of butcher block for my kids, and I settled near the coffee station.

I felt my phone vibrate in my pocket, and after pouring a cup, I pulled it free.

> Laura: Killian just ran in front of us on the way out to the car. He's on the phone with Giles... something is wrong.

My stomach flipped, old worries and fears tugging at the trauma that still lingered in my chest. From childhood, from being taken, from the wars and battles we'd fought over the past ten years. It felt like we never had a break, at least not one that would last.

My father died, and we assumed that meant peace with how many clubs arrived to pay him tribute. We were fools. That display of unity was merely a way of identifying which players still remained in the game, and who would be stepping into which role.

Several clubs had come for us over the years, and many did so because we had little to no alliances left, and far too many grudges to move past. We had the Chaos Kings in our corner, but the Death Raiders were no longer a viable option, even with a good word from Silas. Lance hated Killian and aligned with our enemies. Years passed, and our alliances became fewer and fewer. So this message from Laura had me on edge.

I glanced up and found Natty watching me. Her hands were moving, rounding the dough into balls, while her brows were raised, as if she were waiting for me to tell her what was going on.

Tucking my phone into my back pocket, I walked back over to the counter and slid onto the stool.

"Laura has to put dinner away." I smiled, as if things were okay, but Natty's hands froze in place while her features shuddered.

As much as I didn't want to worry that her being late meant nothing, or that Killian stopping them from coming here was just a precaution, I knew better. So did Natty, which was why I used our code word.

I watched as she slipped her hand under the counter, where I knew she had a knife. Her eyes flicked up to the door at my back and mine moved over to the one that led outside. The knife with the thick black blade moved to the front pocket of her apron.

I tried to think through logistics and safety for those of us in this room. Wes was currently on his way to the club, but Killian had likely already texted him and told him to turn around and come back for us. If he had, he'd likely told Silas as well.

"Mommy, look, I made a snowflake." Ellie smiled at me from where she was standing. Her dark hair was falling out of the braid I had pulled behind her back. Ford was currently shaping a Christmas tree, but I didn't miss the small frown on his face or the way his dark brows furrowed. He looked so much like Wes sometimes that it took my breath away.

The look on his face had me curious if he also knew our little code word that we'd decided to use throughout the years.

Rook flicked a pensive gaze to Ford, and the two seemed to communicate something without saying anything, all while Ellie continued to murmur about her cookie.

The sound of motorcycles echoing down Main Street reverberated outside, which had everyone but Ellie freezing in place. Ford dropped his dough; Rook carefully set his aside, and I stood up slowly, thinking of the gun in my purse.

"I can't wait to decorate this one." Ellie talked quietly, as Ryle moved to stand next to her. His blue eyes remained on his mother, who gave him a little nod. The scent of cinnamon permeated the air as light Christmas music played from the small speaker in the corner of the room. This was supposed to be a fun treat for the kids...it was just days before Christmas and the kids were so excited. Even Ford, with his complaining, had this day circled on the calendar above his desk.

The song switched over to a classic about chestnuts roasting over the fire, which had me taking in a deep calming breath, about to explain that we'd need to leave. But right as I opened my mouth, the kitchen door burst open.

TWO
PENELOPE

"We're already late!" Nova whined for the thousandth time as we made our way toward Main Street. I continued to ignore her, like everyone else in the truck, except Jamie. He kept glancing in the rearview mirror as if part of his heart was being hit each time his little girl complained. I chose to watch the cute storefronts along Main Street begin to bring in their racks of clothes, and the tables that usually sat outside for patrons to enjoy the weather. It was so close to Christmas, they usually left all that out to draw in business, but perhaps there was a cold front coming in or something else.

"Ellie probably took all the best cookie cutter shapes." My daughter tucked her arms in tight, scowling out her window.

My phone vibrated in my lap, but I was half turning in my seat, looking back at Nova to tell her to stop acting so spoiled. She knew how I'd respond to her whining like this. The phone vibrated again as I took in Nova's lighter hair, like Jamie's, but she had my eyes and my mouth. She looked like me, and often acted like me, but at eight years old, she just looked like a little girl, with wide eyes and a heart entirely set on baking Christmas cookies with her best friends.

My heart seemed to soften just like Jameson's had.

"Honey, try not to worry. You know Aunt Natty would never let you miss out on using your favorite cutters, she probably set them—"

My words cut off as the truck slammed to a stop, my chest surging against the seat belt. In the middle of the road was a man on a motorcycle, pointing a gun at our windshield. The air in my lungs wouldn't work, even as a gasp cut through the truck.

Then Jamie was screaming.

"Down, get down. Nova, Connor, get on the floor." He dove over the seat to cover me right as our windshield shattered.

My mind emptied, but then panic swelled, carrying the thoughts I wanted to let drift away, all right back into focus.

We'd been shot at. Someone just shot at our family. My children...my husband.

"Jamie," I breathed with a shuddered breath.

My husband had glass all over his back, but he was okay. I felt him breathing harshly against my neck right as he began to move.

"Don't," I cried, but my husband was already reaching for the gun he kept under the seat. He ensured it was loaded and ready to fire before rasping out a question for our kids.

"Nova, Connor...are you both okay?"

Their voices were small as they replied, "Yeah."

The loud exhaust from a motorcycle began to thrum outside and my gut sank. Whoever had shot at us was now riding toward us.

My daughter began whimpering as Jamie briskly sat up, pointing his gun directly out the center of his window. His brows furrowed as his hand lowered, and the gun was set down on the seat, right before he opened his door and exited the truck.

I slowly sat up, ensuring it was safe while trying to soothe the kids. "Nova, baby, it's okay," I said, but my voice shook. Fear was a hammer battering against my heart.

Jameson walked ahead, meeting a rider in the middle of the road, the man who'd shot at us lay next to his bike on the ground as blood soaked the snowy ground. My husband hugged the rider who was pushing down the kickstand to his bike. From the damage on the shooter's bike, he'd been hit and knocked to the ground.

"Is it safe, Mommy?" Nova asked, and when I looked back, I saw Connor holding her hand while he was trying to peek at what was going on.

"Uncle Giles is out there!" Connor shot up, reaching for his door.

"Connor!" I tried to keep him in place, but he was already leaving and yelling back, "It's the Chaos Kings, they're on our side, Mom."

My son ran around to the front of the truck, where Jameson pulled him under his arm. If the Chaos Kings were here and seemed to know we'd be under attack then that meant only one thing.

My phone buzzed again next to me, and I pulled it up to see a message that had my blood going cold.

> Laura: Dinner is ready, better get back to the club. It's time to eat.

We were at war, and our enemy was already here.

THREE
LAURA

There were many things that made me afraid, especially after becoming a mother. I would lie awake sometimes and ensure I didn't hear anyone trying to break into our home. I would even walk the halls at night like a wraith, and I'd check on my daughters. Once, I even fell asleep between their bedrooms, just drawing circles into the floor until my eyes closed.

Killian found me and carried me back to bed, and then he found me a therapist to help me process the fear.

But that didn't really help anything because it wasn't like I could talk about the things that plagued the Stone Riders. I was the president's wife, and while most clubs didn't include their women in their fights, or the nasty details of what the club had to do to maintain its allies, its runs, and to defend themselves, I knew all of it.

Every sordid detail curled into my head like a shadow monster, reminding of old grudges that might one day come back. Demons that Simon Stone had summoned, that were now ours to defeat. Things we'd walked away from, only to have them return to our front steps.

"I see you're starting to spiral," Killian whispered into my neck, pressing a kiss there.

I'd had the tattoo of a small wolf bite inked into the space where my neck and shoulder met, and my husband never tired of kissing the spot.

My hand came up and ran through his short hair, tugging lightly on the ends to keep him exactly where he was, pressed against my back.

"Why would he come for us now?" I asked, watching as my breath fogged the window. Snow swirled like tiny tornados outside. We lived in the old house that sat on the far part of the property. After renovating the house, our backyard had become one of my favorite places. From our bedroom window, we could see the stone patio, the pergola, the fire pit, and pool. There was a swing set, trampoline and playhouse that our daughters practically lived in.

"There's no guarantee it's him," Killian rasped, pulling me closer to his chest.

I ran my hands over his wrist, and the tattoos he'd gotten since I married him, the little daisies he'd gotten inked there to represent the women in his life.

"It's him, Killian. The least we can do is not pretend."

My husband let out a heavy sigh while running his hand up my torso until he was cupping my breast.

"All I want to do is go back to bed." His lips landed on my skin again, and I closed my eyes. After all this time, his kisses never stopped making me flush, nor did they ever prevent us from making out or taking things too far. Kissing for us was foreplay, no matter where we were or what we were doing.

"Our friends are on their way."

Killian exhaled heavily. "But you're still spiraling."

I was. Our daughters were currently packing little backpacks so we could go stay in the clubhouse until the threat was over. My heart thrashed in my chest at the reminder that this Christmas was going to be ruined if we didn't wear masks for our kids that everything was okay. I had to pull it together for the sake of my daughters. For the sake of everyone.

"I need you to help me relax," I whispered while pushing my husband's wrist. He needed to be lower.

Killian let out a low groan of appreciation before he pulled me away from the window and walked me back toward our bedroom door where he locked it, then lowered to his knees in front of me.

"Whatever you need, Daisy."

His eyes were up on mine as I stroked the silky strands of his hair. He flicked open the copper button of my jeans, then pulled the material down until they were in a small pile on the floor.

"Snowflakes?" Killian looked up and gave me a smile that felt primal.

I let out a small laugh as he stroked up over the material of my thong, and then down my pubic bone, until his large finger was dipping in-between my legs.

On a gasp, I parted my legs and answered him. "It's for Christmas."

"And what else are you going to give me for Christmas?" He gripped behind my thighs and lifted until my legs were over his shoulders, and my back was against the door. His mouth hovered over the apex of my thighs, while his teeth grazed the edges of my thong.

"Do not rip this one, Killian. I bought a whole Christmas set."

His tongue swept up, gliding over the fabric covering my pussy. "A set, huh?"

My fingers pushed through his hair as his tongue continued to trace over the fabric, and then ever so gently, with his eyes on me, he moved my thong to the side, revealing my wet center.

"Looks like you may have ruined these all on your own, Mrs. Quinn. You are soaked, and all from a few swipes over your little Christmas underwear."

"Killian." My moan was more of a breathy plea. Because the way the air was hitting my exposed skin, my soaked slit was aching for him to use that mouth of his and put it to better use.

"I'm worried about ruining your cute little Christmas set. Perhaps I should turn you around and just feast on my other favorite hole. The one that remains so fucking tight because of how infrequent you allow me—"

"Fucking hell, Killian. If you don't fuck me in some way right now."

I felt his laugh everywhere as he leaned in gently and slid his tongue over my clit. He acted as though it was the most tender thing in the world, as if he applied any amount of pressure I'd break. I loved that there were so many sides to him. There were the times he was ravenous, and we fucked hard and fast, and other times when he'd play with me. Those were always my favorite because he'd take his time, and this was one of those times that he seemed to want to play.

"So perfect," he whispered, while fixing his hungry gaze on the space he'd just licked and sucked. He examined it as if he needed to make a plan for where to taste next.

"Killian, we don't have that much time, just fuck me with your tongue so I can come and then if we have enough time, I'll be a good girl and let you finish down my throat."

That must have encouraged him because, suddenly, his hands were on my hips, guiding me closer to him, and then he truly feasted.

I tried to rock my hips, but with my back against the door, I had no leverage, so all I could do was grab his hair and hold tight while he fucked me with his entire mouth.

"Oh my god." I moaned quietly as the curve of his tongue slid up through my slit and circled my clit. He repeated the movement while using his hands to squeeze my ass and pull me closer. He directed the movement, which had me breathing heavily and twisting my body to get more friction. The sound of my wetness filled the room, along with my tiny whines and moans.

My hands went up to my breasts, kneading and cupping them through my thin t-shirt, which I knew would drive Killian crazy. Sure enough, he let out a groan before reaching behind me and pressing his thumb into the bundle of nerves in my ass. It had my breath hitching because while he sucked and licked my pussy, he was pressing hard against the neglected hole, the one he always wanted to access, but I rarely said yes to.

I blamed him, and his freakishly large cock.

The tip of the head was massive, and the few times I did let him access that hole, even lubed up and prepped properly, it burned like a son of a bitch. But the thumb, pressing lightly against it, while he circled my clit, was the perfect combination of pressure and pleasure.

So much so that I tossed my head back, riding his face as much as the door would allow, and then I fell apart. My thighs clenched his face as my orgasm ripped through me, and my husband continued to gently lick up my release, until I was a panting mess, and my legs were completely useless to hold me up.

He gently lowered me to the floor, then reached for his jeans, undoing them. The band of his boxer briefs peeked at me, and while I was still catching my breath, I shifted on my knees and leaned over to pull the elastic down.

The tip of his engorged head was purple and smooth, weeping clear liquid. My mouth parted as my gaze flew up to his. As usual, his hand went to my hair, wrapping it around his fist, and then my mouth was over his length, and I was hollowing my cheeks to try and make more room.

"Fuck," he rasped, gently pushing his hips forward.

I'd sucked his dick thousands of times, probably more over the course of ten years, but each time seemed to feel different. Like there was a new level of hunger that my husband developed for me.

I pulled back and lowered my head to take him again, but he grunted something feral and primal while guiding me by the hair back against the door.

I sat on my heels with my back firmly pressed against the door. My hair was pulled up above my head, so he had a firm hold on me. Then, while he was standing, he stroked his length three times before shifting forward and pressing the head of his dick to my lips.

Keeping my eyes on him, I opened for him and allowed him to fill my mouth, and I knew what he was about to take from me. He wanted to fuck my throat, not my mouth, which was why I was against the door. With one hand gripping my hair, the other was placed against the frame, and then his hips began to move.

His cock pressed deeper into my mouth, hitting the back of my throat until I gagged.

"Yeah, that sound right there. So fucking beautiful, Daisy. My own personal version of 'Jingle Bells.' Do it again."

He pushed back, and I gagged again, my eyes watering while he rocked into me.

My core tightened as my pussy began to grow wet once more, aching with need. I loved this, the intensity, the way he wanted me.

I lifted my hands and gripped the base of him, while allowing him to fuck my mouth the way he wanted. He pushed in hard, then pulled back, and he'd go again. Saliva coated my chin as he pulled out and then forced his way back in, hitting the back of my throat. I sucked his length, hard, and there was an explosion of warmth in my mouth, coating my throat and filling me in ways I couldn't make room for because of his length.

"Look at the mess you're making, Daisy. Still have me hard as fuck with that look in your eyes when I come in that smart mouth of yours."

He pulled out, taking a string of cum with him. The rest dripped down my chin and indeed made a mess. Our eyes connected as he rubbed in the mess, even pushing it back into my mouth. And the tenderness nearly made me cry.

I knew why he'd done this, and that he would continue to do whatever I needed him to so that I felt in control and safe.

We were at war, but my husband was going to make sure all I felt was peace, just like he always did. It made something wake up deep in my bones, this need to protect him too. This need to fight, to stand shoulder to shoulder with him, and make sure our enemies paid.

I smiled up at my husband, stuck my tongue out and relished the smile he returned.

"You ready to go fight, baby?"

I nodded while he pulled me up, and then he kissed me, pinning me to the door and wrapping me in his arms.

When we pulled apart, he whispered, the only words I'd ever need to hear to feel whole.

"I love you, Daisy."

FOUR
NATTY

I STARED AT THE DOOR UNTIL MY EYES STARTED TO WATER.

Rook squeezed my hand, and like usual, I could hide nothing from him. He seemed to know when Callie first made her comment about dinner that it wasn't about food, but instead war. Just like her son Ford did.

And when Wes had barreled into the kitchen with a look of panic on his face, I knew that Silas wasn't with him. My husband had the rare ability to annoy most everyone around him, merely by breathing and scowling, but when he was with the Stone Riders, they all seemed to be a little more at ease. As if they knew, with him on their team, they'd be okay.

Wes didn't look like he had a friend in the whole world that distinct moment his eyes locked on Callie in the kitchen. She'd run into his arms, and his gaze found mine, silently telling me to get my kids and all my things because we were leaving.

Him bursting into the room in a panic meant we were out of time, and there were likely people in town already after us. My theory was proven correct when Wes picked up Ellie and held Callie's hand while walking us through the back door. He'd informed me that I was leaving my car behind and doubling up with Callie. The kids sat two to a seat, and I took the passenger seat while Callie drove, and her husband followed behind us on his bike all the way to the club.

My stomach had been in knots, and I knew Callie's was too by how her fingers continued to shake. She'd push her hair back and give everyone a smile, but I didn't miss how her expression would flick to the door or the picture of her father up on the mantle.

This had been her hell far longer than it was mine. While I had grown up amongst the club, it was different being the daughter of the president, and constantly targeted for who her father was.

"Pen and Jameson aren't here yet," Callie whispered to me, as she took a seat next to me, forcing my eyes away from the door. She had placed warm mugs of hot cocoa in front of the kids, who were watching some holiday movie on the large television screen above the fireplace.

We were in the club, surrounded by members who were being polite enough to give our kids a wide berth. Most of them were on patrol, but any time they walked into the main part of the club, they'd tuck away their weapons and plaster on warm smiles. Ford and Rook seemed to be silently communicating, but Ryle and Ellie were happily watching cartoons while sipping cocoa.

"Mommy, when is Royce and Taryn coming?" Ellie turned her little head of dark hair, asking her mother. Callie was about to reply when the back door to the club opened, and the sounds of little girls' laughter filtered in.

I turned to watch as Killian walked in, holding his daughter Taryn against his chest, her little legs and arms wrapped around him like a koala bear. Then Royce, their oldest, walked hand in hand with Laura. Both girls looked like miniature versions of Laura, with white gold hair and beautiful blue eyes. They could nearly pass for twins, if it wasn't for differences in facial features and ages. Taryn was only seven and her face was more round like Laura's, but Royce was nine, and had her father's features, especially his expressions that often left people unsure if she was planning something or just really pissed off.

"Yay, you're here!" Ellie jumped up and ran over to the girls.

Rook and Ford glanced over, both boys nodding to Royce before smiling at Taryn. Ryle blushed and just sipped his cocoa as if no one had arrived at all.

Laura plopped down next to me and let out a sigh.

"So we're in the thick of it again, ladies. Should we start knitting blankets, you think? That way every time we have to do these little lockdowns, we can remember what was going on in our lives at the time? Like a little time capsule."

"Yes, we should. This time I'd have to learn how to knit being shot at in the middle of the road." Penelope suddenly appeared in the foyer. Her long winter coat was over her fashionable skinny jeans and low-heeled boots, her sweater was thick and her hair perfectly curled. She looked fabulous as always. I jumped up and ran over to her, ensuring she didn't have any bullet holes tucked away under that designer outfit.

"You guys okay?" What did it say about us that her being shot at didn't even surprise me? We had honestly just been through too much shit for any of this to be surprising at this point.

Jameson pushed in after her, holding Nova to his chest, much like Killian had with his daughter. "Giles got him."

I gave Giles a warm smile, wondering if his wife had accompanied him...then registered that he was likely only here because we were in trouble again. Connor, Pen's oldest, stormed in after everyone, his face red as if he were upset. Rook jumped up, same as Ford, and walked over to him, likely to make sure he was okay.

Nova took up residence next to Ellie and Taryn. Royce was watching the older boys with a mildly hurt expression. She was closer in age to the two older boys, closer than even Rook, but they often left her out.

My stomach flipped around like a fish on land, desperate for air. Silas was still out there, and everyone in this room assumed he was in the orchard. No one knew that he was currently in Death Raider territory, visiting Lance after an urgent call had come in this morning from him.

Lance wouldn't betray Silas...but he might betray me. I was the one out of the two of us that identified as a Stone Rider. I was the one that would give my dying breath to save my friends...these people that had become my family. Silas protected them on my behalf, but even ten years later, he still only tolerated them.

It was no secret how he felt about the Stone Riders, even to our sons who loved this place and these people. They knew their father's colors still belonged with the Death Raiders. While Silas didn't fight anymore, didn't even ride for any clubs anymore, I knew deep down, he missed it. Which was why I'd never betray that he was with Lance right now. There was a divide between Lance and Killian, had been for years. It had gotten worse over the last few months…to the point where Killian had asked Silas to pick a side, and my husband merely left the room without saying a word.

"Have they talked about how long we're here, or who is after us?" Penelope asked, pulling off her coat to lay over the back of the couch.

I glanced over at Laura, but she only shook her head before helping her daughter Taryn tie off her braid. Once she was done, she locked eyes with Callie, then me and Pen.

"Let's go make the kids a snack, and I'll tell you what I know."

The three older boys watched as we went; I waved my hand over toward Ryle, making sure Rook understood I wanted him to watch his brother.

The kitchen was clean and quiet as we made our way toward the back pantry area. We'd expanded the space so we could hold more food above just the cellar, since it was so rare any of us would go down there. All these years later, and my heart still throbbed when I looked up and saw the apron we'd pinned next to Red and Brooks' picture. She was still here with us, and sometimes I'd even feel a gust of wind pass me, or something touch my back whenever I was in this kitchen.

I knew if it was anyone, it would be her.

"Killian got a call this morning from Giles. He was yelling, telling us that we needed to pull everyone in," Laura started, keeping her voice low. Callie tucked her arms in close, glancing over at the large opening, past where our kids were.

I thought of the urgent call from Lance, but pushed it aside as Laura continued.

"I was about to leave, but Killian ran in front of me, stopping me. I guess the threat was believed to already be here…it was already in play."

Callie shifted on her feet; her dark brows pulled down. "Do we know who it is?"

Laura glanced at me, and I knew…deep down, I knew it somehow connected back to Silas.

"There are rumors that the men riding today, those coming for us, are wearing colors for a club that we thought had disbanded."

Callie and Pen both swung their heads toward me, while Laura let that hang in the air.

"Who?"

Their stares remained on me, so I spoke of the fear that still kept me up at night on occasion.

"The Destroyers?"

Laura nodded, while Penelope shook her head. "That doesn't make any sense…Fable is dead. Has been for years, who would even lead them?"

Laura's gaze remained on me, accusingly, as if I knew something and wasn't fessing up.

I suppose that were true with my knowledge regarding my husband's affiliations.

Callie looked confused, so did Pen. Then Laura let out a low sigh before stepping closer.

"Did Silas ever speak of another brother?"

FIVE
ROYCE

I hated being left out.

It was worse when I knew Connor wouldn't leave me out if the other boys weren't here. He was my friend, and he always made sure I was included, same with Rook, if it was just the two of us hanging out. Ford didn't seem to care about me one way or another; even if I was included, he didn't seem to mind if I was there.

But when the three of them were together, it seemed as though they couldn't include me because I was a girl. Or maybe it was because they were trying to be like our dads in the club, which didn't have any official girl members. Except my aunt Natty…she was still the only one to this day that was technically a member.

I didn't know what was going on; I just knew it was bad. The last time Mom and Dad pulled us into the club with our friends, and everyone acted like we couldn't leave, I was only seven. The time before that I was five. Now, I was older, and things were changing. For starters, Dad had started teaching me how to shoot, and Mom had given me a laminated map, along with the location to where my grandma lived.

I watched as the boys all laughed in the corner, but I didn't miss how they all kept glancing at the kitchen, then the group standing with my dad by the back wall, where they did Church...Ford, Rook and Connor wanted to know what was going on.

I looked over too. No one was even paying attention to me, so I *could* sneak in there and listen. Besides it wasn't like there was anything to do anyway, and Taryn and I played in this kitchen more than any of the other kids, and I knew where to go where no one would be able to see me.

Right as I stood up and quietly moved toward the hall, my little sister saw and gave me an inquisitive look. Shaking my head, I kept moving toward the wall, so no one would notice me. I heard my mom speaking, her voice was hard and cold, unlike anytime she'd ever talked to me or Taryn.

"Where is Silas? We need to ask him."

She was talking to my aunt Natty. I settled behind the large counter and made sure no one could see me. Natty had her arms crossed and searched the floor while Aunt Callie and Penelope waited for her to speak.

"He's in the orchard."

Mom scoffed, while shaking her head. "You're lying, Nat. I get it. I do... he's your husband, and we would never ask you to put him in harm's way, but we have to ask him."

Natty continued to hold her arms tight against her chest, in a protective stance.

"He's never once mentioned him. Fable had Alec and Silas. He's never mentioned another son."

"He got around though, didn't he? That's how he had Rachel, right? Killian was nearly raised by Fable...so it wouldn't be too far-fetched to assume he had another," Mom said, softer this time.

Natty shook her head. "I don't..."

"Natty, just—"

"Laura, stop. Remember when we did this last time; this isn't the way to get information. I know you're upset and worried, but Natty is ours. She is us. We're on her side no matter what," Aunt Callie said softly. Aunt Pen moved over to put her arm around Natty's shoulders.

I couldn't see Natty's face, but I could see that her eyes were still on the floor.

"Even if it was another son of Fable's, what would that have to do with Silas?" Natty asked.

The group of women were quiet, not responding when Penelope let out a heavy sigh and spoke up.

"Look, she's right. It doesn't matter who is after us. All that matters is that our families are okay. It's two days before Christmas, and our kids are stuck in here, watching holiday movies, while we're all huddled over here, worried. There are no decorations in here, no tree. As hard as it is, it's our job to make this the least scary situation, as we can. We need to focus on them."

Mom rubbed at her forehead, which was something she did when she was frustrated.

"Yeah, you're right. We need to think of them."

The women all turned away, heading toward the entrance of the kitchen, right as two hands grabbed me and pulled me out of my little hiding place and back into the hall.

"What did you hear?" Ford's face was the first I saw, then Rook's.

I pushed them away, which had me falling back into Connor's arms. He helped me stand up, then found my hand and held it. It made me feel safe, like always. Like I had my friend back.

"So, what did you hear?" Ford asked again but then dropped his gaze to where Connor held my hand.

"Something to do with his dad, and a brother no one knew about." I gestured toward Rook.

His blue eyes flashed, only for a second, before he pushed past us.

Ford was on his heels in seconds, pushing him into my mom's office.

"Hey!" Rook yelled, pushing Ford in the chest.

Connor continued to hold my hand as we closed the door.

"So is that true, is your uncle after us?" Ford asked accusingly.

I let Connor's hand go and moved until I was standing in front of Rook. This was what they'd just done to Natty, and I didn't like it.

"Rook is ours. He is us. We don't take sides against the club."

Ford scoffed. "His dad isn't even in the club."

"His mom is, and that's all that matters," I replied.

Connor glared over my shoulder, while Rook glared back. Ford didn't move and my heart began pounding fast. They were best friends. I hated that this was dividing us.

"Our moms decided that all that mattered right now was each other.

Us. They want to put together a good Christmas for all of us. Especially the younger kids. I think we should focus on helping with that."

All three boys were quiet, but I saw that Rook's fists were clenched tight.

"Come on, let's go see if we can help find a tree, or something to liven this place up. Our parents are handling all the bad guy stuff." Connor finally relented and opened the door.

SIX
KILLIAN

My men kept glancing at each other like they weren't sure the order I gave was real.

"Sir, did we understand you correctly?"

"You did." I smiled at Orson.

The freshly pledged member rubbed at the back of his neck.

"Sir, I've never been a Santa before."

Orson wasn't even the best pick, but he'd recently pissed Harrison off well enough that I stuck him with this task. I knew it was going to push him out of his comfort zone and truly test how loyal he was.

"First time for everything, Orson. Now, Harrison went and found you a suit to wear and everything. All you need to do is dress up and show up."

A few of the other members laughed, while Orson's brown eyes scanned the backyard. We were standing a few feet away from the house because my beautiful wife decided she wanted to take the kids to go tree hunting. I informed her that she would not be doing that, but instead, said that one of my men would go and chop down the biggest one he could find on the property.

Laura argued, and then suggested we just bring the tree from our living room over.

I argued back, which led to us taking a fifteen-minute break where we locked ourselves inside of a bathroom, and I fucked her against the wall.

I won. Yeti was out locating an acceptable tree to bring back for the kids. The rest of us were on watch. Wes was behind me somewhere, silently being the vice president of our club, just like he always was. He was my biggest support system, but the man didn't say shit about shit unless it was absolutely required of him.

Giles had explained what had prompted his phone call this morning, but my mind was still trying to piece together exactly what it all meant. Since the Chaos Kings were currently our only ally, I was careful not to grill my friend too harshly. He'd arrived just in time to intervene for his cousin, Jameson and their family. I was grateful to him, but I still didn't understand how he knew about the threat before we did.

Or where the fuck Silas was.

"I know Callie is going to ask for specifics." Wes locked his eyes on me while talking to Giles. He was doing it for my benefit, and mine only. He knew I couldn't ask a million questions without it seeming like I didn't trust the information Giles had given us.

"Anyway you can go back through it, Giles?"

Giles still had that stocky look to him, with lighter hair, and a softer, almost innocent expression about him that typically put people at ease. He'd transitioned through a few vice presidents over the years, but whoever held the helm currently was still in Richland.

"Look, I get it. The holes in the story were only going to hold things off for so long, I get that. I knew you'd need more. The truth is, if I tell you, you have to promise not to get pissed off at me."

My eyes flew to Wesley's, who was silently communicating with me to tread carefully.

Yeah, fuck that. My family was inside, and we were now essentially fish in a fucking barrel.

"Start talking, Giles."

With a heavy sigh, the president of the Chaos Kings took a seat on the retaining wall. His breath clouded in front of him, which had me looking up at the sky. Snowflakes swirled around our heads and then landed gently on the stone holding up the grass and mud.

"I have an alliance with the Death Raiders."

Fucking hell. I wasn't expecting that…

Wes crossed his arms. "Since when?"

"Two months ago…I met with Lance…and…" He paused, wincing the smallest bit, which had Wes staring at me. I knew what he was thinking because I was thinking the same thing.

"And who?"

Giles kicked at the frozen dirt while my men walked around, checking the perimeter. Yeti was still looking for a tree. My walkie and cell rested next to me on the top of the wall while I waited for the next shoe to drop.

"Silas." Giles exhaled, then added quickly, "But it's not what you think…he hasn't turned or anything."

Wes dropped his chin to his chest while I scoffed. "Hard to turn when you never pledged or committed to begin with."

Suddenly Jameson stepped outside, his leather jacket covering his shoulders. It had on his colors for our club, but that didn't mean he wasn't still sympathetic to what his old club dealt with. I had to assume Silas felt the same way. The difference was Jameson had pledged to the Stone Riders and wore his loyalty on his chest and back. Silas never had, except to prove his loyalty to his wife.

But Natty was loyal to Silas in a way that surpassed her loyalty to the club. Even more so now that they had two children together. Laura told me she'd already questioned Natty earlier, but she wasn't giving anything away.

"Keep going, Giles. Tell us about this meeting with Lance and Silas." I nodded toward Jameson to join us. He rubbed his hands together and took a seat on the retaining wall.

"Kids are okay in there?" I lifted an eyebrow, and he nodded.

"Natty started baking cookies in the kitchen with them."

Giles checked his phone, which had me on edge.

"I made an alliance with Lance because about two months ago, we had something happen up in Richland that caused a stir."

Wes kicked his foot out, crossing one ankle over the other. "What sort of stir?"

"The kind that hit the Death Raiders first. Ten of their members were killed in a way that sent a message. It was out of the blue. It shook Lance, so much so that he brought Silas into it."

Jameson was the one who asked, "Why would Silas need to be brought into it?"

Giles rubbed his hand over his head then exhaled once more. "Because the calling card left behind was the same one left with mine. They took seven of my members, and those men all had families."

"Who is *they*?" Wes asked, glancing around our little group.

Giles looked each of us in the eye when he said the one word that had me going back in time ten years, the last time I thought we might lose everything. The only other time I honestly felt like we might not make it out alive.

"The Destroyers."

SEVEN
CALLIE

Mercer and Yeti walked in carrying a massive six-foot pine tree. It wasn't as full or as aesthetically beautiful as one that we would get from a tree lot, or even hiking out in the forest to find ourselves, but it was tall and green and most importantly, the kids loved it.

"We have a tree!" Ellie yelled excitedly.

The hours had dwindled, and it was getting closer to dinner time. Penelope had Connor in the kitchen with her, along with Ford and Royce who were all helping chop potatoes while Natty was adding chicken and rice into a large pot. The room smelled divine, and I knew the kids had hit their limit of being cooped up in one space.

"Who's ready to help me find some Christmas decorations?"

Ryle, Nova, Taryn and Ellie all stood excitedly. Yeti and Mercer managed to find a way for the tree to have a base, using a few tools from the garage that still sat off to the far side of the club. While they worked, I held out my hand toward the kids and wandered to Laura's office with all the kids in tow.

My best friend was at her desk, typing furiously on her laptop. Her dark brows were furrowed, her hair was in wild waves of gold down her back, and while I knew she was doing something for the club, I also knew that mother's heart in her chest needed to be a part of what we did next.

"Laura, do you think you can find us some flashlights or headlamps? We need to go hunting for Christmas decorations."

Pushing away from her desk, Laura beamed and gently closed her laptop. "Oh my, that sounds like an awfully big adventure. Can I join you?"

"Yes, join us, Mommy!" Taryn left our little line of hand holding and ran toward her mother. Laura opened her arms and scooped her daughter into a tight hold.

"Flashlights would be in the cellar of all places, but I think we have a few in here somewhere." Laura glanced around the room and stalled on the far side of it, where Killian's desk sat.

"Taryn, can you go look in the bottom drawer of your daddy's desk?"

With a huge smile, Taryn ran over and pulled the bottom drawer open. "There's one in here!"

Laura slid the bottom drawer open near her leg and sifted through a few things before bringing out another flashlight that matched the one her daughter had found.

"Daddy and I sometimes play hide and seek in the dark." Laura laughed as she turned on her light and flashed it at her daughter. Taryn tried to do the same, but the button wouldn't click.

"Here, Aunt Callie. You can carry it, it's too hard for me." Taryn walked over to me, placing the large metal light in my hand.

I smiled over at Laura who joined me, and together, we clicked the butt end of our lights against one another and walked toward the stairs that would lead us up to the attic.

"Are there really decorations up here?" Ryle asked, trailing as we hit the very top level of the house.

"There's a few lights, but honestly I'm not sure what else. I haven't been up here in a long time." I smiled at him then twisted the knob to the door, while Laura clicked on her light.

"I'm scared," Ellie said, clinging to my arm. Nova joined her, holding onto my other side.

"There's nothing to be afraid of up here, except dust and maybe spiders," I mused while walking farther into the attic until I found the light switch.

The room illuminated, showing bookcases against the wall, a card table, two folding chairs, an old radio and a bottle of whiskey on the other side of the room.

"Let's dig through a few of these boxes." We all moved toward the edge of the space. Ryle peeked from behind me as Nova did the same, until she moved and picked up a box all on her own.

"I see Mickey Mouse!"

My face flushed as an old memory surfaced of when I was seven and begged my father to buy me all Mickey Mouse themed Christmas decorations. He didn't have the money for it, but Red had found a whole box at a garage sale. It was one of the best Christmases I ever had because the snow was intense, my father couldn't ride, and at the time he couldn't afford any other form of transportation. So he remained home with me, Killian, Red and Brooks. It felt like we were just a little family, no club, no one else to steal my father from me.

"There's an entire box full of Mickey, Minnie and," Ellie began pulling out piece by piece and shrieked when she found my Cinderella star that went on the top of the tree.

"Cinderella!"

"Is there anything in here that's not for babies?" Ryle asked, pulling another box out.

Lord knew what he might find up here; in retrospect, this was a terrible idea.

"Hang on, wait for me to look in there." I helped him open it, but it was just a bunch of Killian's old things from when he was a kid. Ryle smiled as he pulled out a few action figures and a toy motorcycle.

He dropped the action figures and immediately started driving the bike around the room, along all the surfaces. Laura took the box with gentle hands and began sifting through it, gently pulling tiny little items out, one at a time, with a dreamy smile on her face.

"Do you think he'll let me keep this?" Ryle asked, holding his hand out, while he maneuvered the toy up the wall and around the thick wooden trim.

Taryn's head popped up as she huddled around her mother. "There are two! I'll have one and you'll have one, Ryle. We can match."

Laura smiled. "Ryle, I'm sure Killian would love for you to have that."

Taryn moved until she was right next to Ryle, the two of them moving their toy bikes at the same pace across the folding table.

"We will have to keep it for always, Ryle. Promise."

Ryle was quiet for a moment, just making little engine sounds when he finally replied, "Okay. I promise."

From downstairs, someone yelled that dinner was ready, so I pulled the Mickey box up and encouraged everyone to follow me back down. Laura fell into step next to me as the kids headed back down the stairs ahead of us. On a whispered tone, she said, "It's the Destroyer's. Giles confirmed it."

My stomach felt like concrete, as though the next blow would land like a sledgehammer and make me crumble to pieces. My fingers tightened around the box, digging into a corner so hard, I knew blood might be drawn if I kept pressing.

"How is that possible?" I whispered back.

Laura shook her head as we descended more steps and cleared the third floor then moved to scale the next section, lowering us to the second story.

"Silas is still missing. He has to know something…we need to figure out where he is. It doesn't make sense that he'd leave Natty and the boys here."

I silently agreed with her as we neared the last staircase, which would take us to the bottom floor. The scent of chicken and vegetables, butter and bread permeated the air, making my stomach growl. Laughter flitted up like a cheery jingle from the back of the kitchen, where the older kids were playing. Killian, Wes and Jameson were back there with them, all having a whip cream fight.

The younger kids ran to join them, as Laura remained next to me, continuing our conversation.

"Laura, I know you're feeling worried, but it is possible that Natty doesn't know and is twice as panicked as we are. I'm not willing to risk my friendship with her just to figure out where he is. Silas would die before he ever let anything happen to them, which means if he isn't here, then they're safe. Let's take comfort in that."

I squeezed her hand tight then broke away, wishing I could believe the words I just said.

EIGHT
NATTY

My sons smiled as they ate, a rosy glow filling their cheeks. I tried to take those expressions and the way they laughed as a form of hope. I willed the feeling to replace the fear and panic curling in my lungs and filling my stomach. My fingers trembled as I sipped my water, and I felt Laura's gaze linger on my back.

Callie was watching too, even if her expression was more pity than anger. Killian and Wes glanced my way from time to time as well, and I knew they all wanted to know where my husband was. I wanted to know more than even they did. But Silas always had a reason for what he did, and while it had been years since he'd had to deal with club politics, or challenges, I clung to what I knew of my husband and his character.

He was ensuring our safety. It was a good thing if he wasn't here. It meant he felt like we were safe, but it didn't change how uncomfortable it made me to have my friends question him, and me by extension.

"Mom, will you help us decorate the tree?" Ryle asked, while Rook swung his gaze over to the tree then back to his brother.

"I'll help."

Ryle was holding a tiny metal motorcycle toy, but I had no idea where he found it.

I stood up and held my hand out to both my boys. "Let's go start unpacking the decorations."

We moved toward the open space where the couches formed a square around the large mantle place. The large television mounted above it was playing an older Christmas movie about Frosty the Snowman. There was a fire burning in the hearth, making a warm glow. The crackle from the logs had me releasing a shuddery sigh.

This was nice. My sons were safe; they were smiling.

Ryle opened the box and gently pulled out a bundle of large bulbed Christmas lights.

"They're all tangled." Rook pulled another pile out, and the two started separating the wires. I was about to get down to help when suddenly a loud banging came from outside. My gaze moved to the windows a few stories up; dusk spread across the sky with just the smallest bit of light. Enough to show the snow that was falling sideways against the glass in thick waves of white.

Someone burst in through the door at the back, which had me spinning around.

Yeti and Mercer walked in, both of them brushing their bushy beards free of the snow covering them from head to toe.

Right before they explained what we all already knew, a loud alarm went off on my phone, then like a chain reaction, everyone's phones blared with a similar sound.

"What's wrong, Mom?" Rook asked, crowding over my shoulder.

I found Penelope's gaze from across the room, and then moved to Callie and Laura's.

"It's an alert, Buddy."

Ryle moved to my lap and tried to see my phone. "An alert for what?"

I glanced back up at the windows above us and tried to keep my tears at bay as I answered him.

"A blizzard."

NINE
CONNOR

My mom and dad were too quiet.

I knew them well enough now from family vacations that Dad snored and Mom mumbled in her sleep. Usually about something Nova was doing, or my dad, but I had never heard her sleep yell at me for anything, so I assumed I was her favorite.

But tonight, neither of them was making any noise.

We were all placed into different rooms; our family was given the downstairs basement area, which had pool tables, a few couches, and really soft carpet. I was on the floor in a sleeping bag, right next to my little sister, and my parents were on the pull-out couch, huddled close and from the sounds of it, whispering.

I held my breath, trying to listen. Thankfully down here the wind from the storm wasn't as bad, and it was warm from the water heater or something like that. Dad explained it, but I wasn't listening.

Not like now. I was right below their feet, so I should be able to hear them if I just…

"I can't stop worrying that this is going to be the worst Christmas for our kids, and I know I'm being selfish, but they're the ones I'm most worried about," Mom whispered.

I heard my dad kiss her then reply, "They're going to be okay, Pen. We're together and that's all that matters."

"I know, but they're not going to have any decorations or presents. Why can't we leave and at least go to our house to grab a few things?"

I perked up at that. I really wanted to get my Nintendo Switch, and if we could at least go home to grab a few things, it would make all of this so much easier.

My dad waited a second then responded with a sigh. "Pen, they shot at us. On the road, in the middle of the day, while our kids were in the car. They knew where we were going to be…they are watching our homes. Which is why we're here. We can't go back, not until we know it's safe."

My mom seemed to accept that because they stopped whispering, and after a few minutes, they both seemed to fall asleep. Dad was snoring, and Mom was breathing in a way that told me she was out. I couldn't seem to fall asleep, so I slid out of my sleeping bag and quietly walked toward the stairs.

I wasn't even sure what I was going to do, but I knew that I wanted to walk around for a second. Maybe see if I could find some way to help with decorations. The door at the top of the stairs opened on quiet hinges as I slipped out. The howling from the wind was the first thing I heard. It was eerie and creepy, especially with all the lights off.

I always thought it was funny that this was supposed to be a dangerous motorcycle club, but any time us kids came around, it turned into an extra-large house that we were allowed to run and play in. No one so much as cussed around us, or at least hadn't in a very long time. Most of the members became scarce when us kids were here, and I remember back when I was little, things weren't always like that. Members used to stay, hang out, and me and Ford would just hang with them.

It wasn't until that first attack after we were born that things stopped.

A creak on one of the stairs had me twisting around in a panic, but Royce was slowly making her way down the staircase, her finger up to her lips, telling me not to be loud.

"What are you doing?" I whispered as she got closer. She wore her unicorn pajamas that Ford made fun of her for being too old for. I liked them though, mostly because they were familiar. She'd been wearing unicorns on her pajamas since we were five years old; they were her favorite animal, even if they weren't real.

Royce moved closer to me, ducking as if she didn't want to be seen. "I wanted some water, what are you doing up?"

"I don't know, can't sleep."

There was another creak from the opposite side of the house, and Ford crept out from where his parents were staying. Once upon a time, there was an apartment on the other side of the club, but Uncle Killian did something to it. From what I remember, he just made it to where the apartment was inside the club, all connected now.

"What are you guys doing?"

Royce let out a sigh before crossing her arms. It bothered me that the two of them didn't get along. They were my best friends, but the older we got, the more it seemed they hated being around each other.

Ford walked past Royce, hitting her shoulder as he went.

"Hey!" I whisper-yelled at Ford, but Royce gently pulled on the back of my shirt to get me to stop. I didn't want to though. Not with the way Royce had nearly lost her footing.

Suddenly Rook appeared out of nowhere, silent as ever.

"What are we sneaking?"

Ford and Royce froze, while I pushed past the two of them and walked into the kitchen.

"I think there's cookies in the pantry." I clicked the overhead light in the large storage room and scanned the shelves.

The other three came over, and the four of us began searching the space for cookies. My foot shifted, emanating a creak from below us, which had all of us pausing and looking down.

"The old cellar," Royce whispered, bending low to trace her finger over the small outline of a door.

Rook mirrored her movement and then I did too. I slightly remembered the cellar...but it had been years.

Royce reached for the metal handle. "We should see if there's any Christmas decorations down there. Maybe cheer up the kids after the Mickey Mouse ones didn't work."

"We could get in trouble if anyone comes looking," Ford said, looking around.

Rook moved to help while waving us off. "We can just tell them we were looking for more blankets."

Rook pulled up, and Royce helped him lift the door. Lights flicked on underneath, lighting up the concrete floor and wooden steps leading down into the cellar.

"You go first. It was your big idea." Ford nudged Royce, but she elbowed his arm in return.

"I'm not afraid." Her bare feet hit the first step, and I rushed to join her.

She turned her head, her blonde hair flying as she looked at my hand that was now holding hers. She stopped walking, but I kept going. "I said I'm not afraid."

I ignored her, scaling the steps until we'd reached the very bottom.

"I know."

Rook and Ford followed after us, and once we were on the floor, we collectively stared at the large shelves and boxes around the room.

"Where do we even start looking?" Royce asked, with a slight tremble in her voice.

The floor was freezing, so I knew she had to be cold.

Letting her hand go, I moved to one of the storage shelves, inspecting all the supplies. Rook and Ford moved around to different parts of the cellar, sifting through things.

"Do you remember who Red was?" Ford asked, poking through a large box.

I turned toward them, shaking my head. "I think she died before any of us were old enough to meet her."

"Isn't this you, Connor?" Ford held up a framed photo of a baby being held in some woman's arms who had white hair and a huge smile. My mom was next to her, so was Aunt Natty.

"That is me."

Royce moved in, looking over my shoulder. "So you did know her then."

I wanted to trace the woman's smile because the way she was looking down at me, she must have loved me.

"There are more pictures in here," Rook said, sifting through a box. I started digging through it too, seeing picture after picture of this woman with my family. It made me wonder about back then, when things were different. When my mom and dad were just getting together from what they told me, at least. Dad had once told me all of it. The whole story about where I came from, the club he once led. The club my biological dad sabotaged and the way they had to come to the Stone Riders for help.

Just then, the wind started blowing, but the whistling came through part of the back wall behind the shelves.

"What is that?"

Ford moved first, walking down the hallway between two tall shelves as the whistling sound picked up.

"There's a door back here...or at least there used to be," Ford called from his spot behind the shelves. We all moved until we were behind him, crowding the small piece of wall that was boarded up, save for a sliver of space where cold air was blowing through.

Royce pressed her fingers into the crack, and Ford watched the side of her face with a grim expression.

"They boarded up whatever used to be here, but it wasn't sealed off."

Rook bent down and pulled the rug away from where we were standing. "The whole floor is just cold cement, except right here. Why would they put a rug here?"

He pushed the rug back, revealing a small wooden hatch cut into the floor.

Rook glanced up and around at all of us before tossing the rug behind him. "So a secret door that's sealed, and now a secret door in the floor?"

Royce knelt down next to him. "Looks like the door that we came through for the cellar."

Her blue eyes moved up until they were locked on me. Then Rook followed, as if they were both waiting for me to say something.

"Why are you looking at me?"

"You're the oldest," Rook said, but Ford clicked his tongue.

"By like two months."

I crouched down and pulled on the metal handle, but it wouldn't budge.

Royce was about to move in to help me, but Ford nudged her out of the way.

"Pull harder."

Ford grunted as his shoulders heaved. "I'm trying."

"Maybe we aren't supposed to open it, maybe whatever is in there we aren't supposed to see," Royce said, placing her hands on top of the wood.

Right as she said it, we heard someone call for us from above the cellar.

We all straightened while Rook quickly moved the rug back over the floor.

"Let's go." I held my hand out for Royce, but she ignored it. I glared at her while she walked past me. Ford watched our interaction while running past Royce, so he was the first to exit the stairs. I had no idea why my stomach felt weird watching it, but for some reason, I knew Ford rushed up there to make sure Royce didn't get in trouble.

I looked down and pushed the weird feeling away, maybe they were finally going to be friends? That would be good.

But why did the feeling seem so bad?

TEN
ROOK

The room was dark when I snuck back inside.

Mom once told us that she'd lived in this place, and all these years later, there were still a few things of hers here. It made me wonder if my dad knew about it, or if maybe he came to visit this place with her, or maybe it was for her and my aunts. She liked to have time with them and it wasn't very often they came out to the Orchard.

"What were you doing out there, Rook?" my mom whispered from her place on the bed.

I stood close to the edge of where she was sleeping, but her eyes were open. Sometimes my mom reminded me of an angel. Her hair was fair and wispy, and pieces always curled against her face. She was always happy. Even when she was mad, she only stayed that way for a few minutes before she was smiling again.

"I went looking for cookies."

She patted the space next to her, and I crawled in beside her. She pulled me closer, hugging me while pressing a kiss to the back of my head.

"Cookies?"

"Didn't find any though." I smiled in the dark, listening to Ryle breathe on the couch across the room.

"What did you find, Little Bird?"

I wasn't sure if I should tell her, but Mom never got mad at us for being curious. "We went into the cellar and found a secret hatch in the floor."

Mom froze behind me, which made me even more nervous about what was under there.

"Did you open it?"

I shook my head. "No."

Mom's fingers slowly slid in my hair as she let out a heavy sigh. Things were quiet for a minute until I finally asked the thing that had been on my mind since this morning.

"How come Dad isn't here yet?"

She continued to stroke my hair until finally she softly replied, "Daddy had to go help Uncle Lance with something this morning."

"Mom, I'm not a baby...you can tell me what's going on."

She was quiet again, but this time, she moved until I was sitting up and she was sitting next to me.

"Honestly, I don't know. But I know your dad would be here if he could, but the fact that he's not means we're safe. You know that."

I did know that. Dad would never leave us if he thought we might be in trouble.

"But why can't we just leave and go home?"

Her fingers found mine and she gently squeezed.

"Tenebrae iterum nos invenit. Non solum opus est ut omnem lucem protegat." *Darkness has found us again. We just need to protect all the light.*

I pulled my hand away, frustrated that she wasn't just telling me. She always got cryptic when she spoke in Latin. Maybe I was just tired, but I felt tears burn the backs of my eyes. I wanted to go home. And I wanted my dad.

My mom probably sensed my mood, and where it was taking me, because right as I moved to leave her bed, she lightly gripped my wrist.

"If I were you, I'd check the cabin. Make sure the grounds are safe first, and the blizzard has to have died down, but there might be a clue about that secret hatch you found out there."

"It's snowing again," Royce said from off to the left. Her nose was pressed against the glass, just like mine.

I was watching the members of the club blow hot air into their palms, while walking along the perimeter of the property, when Royce Quinn randomly sat next to me. I was just waiting for the right moment to ask them to go to the cabin with me.

"Yeah, there's a lot of it out there too."

But not as much as I assumed would be out there after the blizzard warning.

Royce turned toward me and gently put her hand on my shoulder.

"You worried about your dad?"

My stomach turned over like I was sick, but I just shook my head.

"I'm sure he's fine."

The sounds of Christmas music filled the air from the television where the younger kids were snuggled up on the couch, under blankets. We all woke, and it felt like the heat hadn't been on all night. Mom explained how hard it was to heat the main area of the club because of how big it was. The fire was roaring, but it was still chilly.

"What are you guys looking at?" Ford came up next to us, staring out the window.

"I want to go to the cabin…I think there might be another door there. We could look for more Christmas lights too."

"We can go out through the kitchen door. The one that no one ever uses." Royce stood up, watching her mom and mine cook in the kitchen.

Ford turned away, checking the stairs. "I'll go get Connor."

Royce and I headed into the kitchen through the side hall, closest to her mom's office. Aunt Laura didn't see us walking, but my mom did. She gave me a wink before returning to kneading the bread in front of her.

I pulled on my coat and boots, so did Royce, and once Connor and Ford met us, we left through the back door.

The wind hit my face, icy and frigid. Snow swirled above our heads, but the wind wasn't blowing like it was last night.

We started walking, lifting our legs high to clear the snow that had built up. Ford looked over at Connor, and the two of them followed. The cabin was sort of far from the main club, but we must have all just silently agreed we could manage, even with the snow. Except, by the time we reached it, we were all breathing heavily and our cheeks were red from the cold.

"This was a stupid idea," Royce complained while stomping her boots on the porch.

Ford followed suit, stomping all the snow off.

Connor glared around the space, frowning at the boarded-up windows. Something had happened out here a few years back. I wasn't sure what, or couldn't remember, but it had to do with someone trying to hurt my aunt Laura and uncle Killian.

"Do we even know if it's unlocked?"

I hadn't even thought of it being locked. Warmth invaded my face as I reached the steps and joined everyone waiting by the door.

Connor must have read my expression because he pulled on the screen door without dragging out the issue.

"One way to find out."

His hand wrapped around the brass knob and twisted. The door opened with a low creak, but Connor had to use his shoulder to push it all the way open.

"I don't think anyone has been out here in a long time," Ford said, assessing the room. The light from outside came in through the windows along the back of the cabin. There was a round table in the small dining area, but the space was smaller than I imagined.

"How did anyone even live in here," Connor asked, lightly kicking at the pinkish couch. It could only fit two people. Connor's comment made me want to roll my eyes. He was rich and spoiled. He and his sister had everything they could ever want, plus a huge house, on a ton of property. They even had a pond in their backyard.

Even Ford and Royce, they all had big houses. But Ryle, Mom, Dad and me, we all lived in a small cottage up in the orchards. We loved it. Ryle and me, we shared a room, always have, but I wouldn't have it any other way. I liked that we didn't have a ton of space, made it so I always knew where my dad and my mom were. They loved that house, and every square inch of it was full of love.

Royce moved over to the bedroom off to the side. "There's a closet, might be some decorations."

Connor was next to her within seconds, just like I knew he would be. Even Ford shook his head, moving in the opposite direction. While they looked, I began searching the floors for any sort of door that matched the one I saw in the cellar.

By the wood stove, I pulled back the rug there, but found nothing. I checked the kitchen, under the table, and even ended up moving the couch. Nothing.

I was starting to doubt my mom when Royce called for us from the room, "Hey, come look at this."

Ford and I looked at each other then quickly moved to where the other two were.

There, under the window where Royce and Connor were huddled, was a small hatch that matched the one we'd found last night.

"So it's true," I whispered, moving closer to it.

Connor's eyebrows shot up. "You knew?"

"It's why I wanted to come out here. I just wanted to see if there was a chance the two connected." I didn't want to tell them I'd told my mom, because they'd probably get mad at me and call me a snitch.

Ford crouched and placed his hand on the silver handle. "You ready to see what's under here?"

Royce backed up the smallest bit. "I still think maybe we aren't meant to know."

"The wood is newer than the original floors," I pointed out, running my hand over the smooth surface.

Ford followed my gaze. "So?"

"So, whatever this is…it's been made recently."

Royce stared at me, then the hatch. "So nothing super old and haunted then."

"Probably not," Connor mused, before pulling on the silver handle. But the hatch wouldn't budge.

"Maybe we aren't strong enough?" I asked, narrowing my gaze at the frustrating door. Why hadn't my mom warned me that we wouldn't be able to open it?

Royce shook her head. "I'm taking this as a sign. Let's check the other closet for decorations."

I actually agreed with her this time. Whatever the door was, maybe it was better if we just left it alone. Right as I stood up, Connor pulled once more on the door, grunting as he went, until suddenly he was gasping, and Ford was muttering a curse word his mom told him not to say.

The hatch was open.

ELEVEN
ROYCE

I spun around right as Ford and Connor faced the small hatch, both of them staring down inside it. For some reason my heart seemed to beat a thousand times a minute as both Rook and I slowly turned and approached them.

I didn't want to know what was in that hole. Whatever it was, I felt like it would have been better for all of us if we just didn't know. My mom sometimes talked about club secrets, and how once upon a time she had to see every single one of them, and how even now, years later, there were some things she couldn't unsee. She talked about how sometimes, it was just better not to know.

"What is it?" Ford asked, crouching once more to inspect the hole.

Connor seemed engrossed, which made my stomach churn with nervousness. He seemed too excited and not nearly afraid enough.

"I think it's a tunnel," Connor said, in awe.

Rook glanced over at me with the same expression that I knew I wore on my face. This wasn't something we should even know about, much less be looking down into.

"It must connect to the main club," Connor said, like he was adding up an equation.

So I offered my two cents. "Guys, we should close that and get back."

Connor glanced back at me then down at the pack he'd brought. I knew what he was going to do, and I felt like I wanted to cry.

"Connor, don't." I started forward, but Ford caught me at the waist.

"If he wants to go, then let him."

Connor gave me a big smile. "I just want to see if it connects."

"But what if it was never finished, or it's unstable. What if it caves in?" My voice was raspy as I tried to push forward again. If I could just grab his hand then I could talk sense into him.

"It'll be fine. It's deep enough that a cave-in isn't a concern. If it's not finished, I'll just turn around and head back."

Rook glared at where Ford was holding me and I knew he didn't like it. No one really liked how Ford treated me, and while he wasn't hurting me, he was stopping me from saving Connor from making a huge mistake.

"What about air? You won't be able to breathe."

Ford released me and pulled out a metal lighter from his back pocket, making my eyes narrow. Why would he even be carrying that?

He quickly climbed down the ladder and then slid his thumb over the starter, igniting the flame. It flickered as if a breeze was blowing through the tunnel.

"There's got to be a vent somewhere, but air won't be an issue," he yelled back up at us.

Fear swelled like a balloon again, this time nearly suffocating me. Ford climbed back up and put his metal lighter back into his rear pocket.

"It's dark down there."

"Someone is going to have to be on the other side to open the hatch for you," Rook finally said, after staring at the opening.

I walked over to Connor and pulled his wrist.

"Please don't go. This is really dangerous, and I'm worried about you."

I knew I was younger than Connor, and he looked at me like a baby sister, but I really hoped he'd hear the fear in my voice and choose to see me as a friend.

His blue eyes flickered, as if he felt remorse, but he blinked and it was gone.

"I'll take my pack. It has a flashlight, glow sticks I can throw ahead and behind, and a walkie talkie."

"Who has the other walkie?" I looked over to Rook, then Ford.

Ford raised his hand. "But it's back at my house."

"Great." I crossed my arms. "So, no one can talk to you while you're down there."

Connor grabbed his pack and pulled out the flashlight. I glanced down at the hole in the floor. Below the floorboard was more wood that rounded as a border and a solid ledge for the ladder to attach to. The rungs went down, deep into the packed dirt. Whoever created this tunnel had taken an extraordinary amount of care in making sure it was done well.

"Toss one of your glow sticks down, so we can see how far down it goes," I said, hoping the depth would discourage him. To my surprise once the light hit the bottom, it wasn't that far, and it didn't seem nearly as deep or intimidating.

"See, piece of cake."

"Still, it's dangerous, Connor," I begged him to see reason.

His flashlight was out, and before I could say anything else, my best friend was crawling down inside the hole.

"Shut this hatch, then you guys get back to the club and help me out over there."

My mind was racing nearly as fast as my heart. Everything about this situation was screaming at me to make him stop. This wasn't a fun game; this was him going underground just to see where the tunnel went.

Right as I was about to open my mouth, Rook stepped forward.

"I'm going too."

Some of the pacing eased as I swung my eyes over to his dark hair and light eyes.

Connor watched him, then flicked a gaze over at Ford.

"Cool, we'll meet you guys there."

Ford hesitated. "Maybe I should go too."

"I need someone to help me lift the hatch in the cellar!" I cried, nearly hyperventilating over these idiots.

Ford gave out a sigh, like I was so irritating to him, but gave me a small nod.

Connor and Rook slowly made their way down into the hole, and once they were on the ground, they gave us a salute before walking forward and out of view. Ford slowly lowered the hatch until it was sealed closed.

Then he stood and looked at me, like he wasn't sure what to do with me.

"We better get back in time to help them out. Without the snow down there, they'll move faster."

I moved behind him, exiting the cabin the same way we'd come in, and tucked my hands under my armpits. The air was frosty and cold as we started walking again. I didn't want to walk all the way back when the air felt this cold against my face.

My knees felt too small to clear the snow, which was crazy because I couldn't even remember the last time we'd had this much snow. Every Christmas was usually spent hoping for snow, but accepting a bit of frost that liked to coat the trees.

We walked for what felt like ten minutes before I finally broke the silence between us.

"How come you stopped me from reaching him?" I asked, keeping my eyes ahead and ignoring how red my nose was getting.

Ford glanced over, but kept walking.

"Didn't want you to fall in."

Liar. I rolled my eyes, knowing he couldn't see me.

"I wouldn't have fallen in."

Ford scoffed. "You're clumsy. I think you would have then we'd all get in trouble, and your dad would come down here and see that his perfect daughter was hurt. Then we'd be in trouble, just like we always got in trouble as kids."

"We're still kids," I offered, huffing out a breath.

"You're a kid. I'm almost a teenager." I saw him pointing at his chest out of the corner of my eye.

"You're not almost a teen, you're like ten, Ford."

"I'll be eleven in a few months," he argued back, stepping closer to my side of the field. Our tracks were nearly matching, our strides too. Even though he was much taller.

"Connor will be eleven sooner than you." I wasn't sure why I said it. It didn't matter, and it wasn't like the two of them were in a competition. I just hated how bossy and prideful he got over being older. It drove me nuts. Especially when he didn't even act his age half the time. I acted older and definitely more mature.

Ford stared ahead, not saying anything until finally his shoulder bumped mine but not in a friendly way. "And how old are you, Royce, not even ten years old yet."

"I'm—"

He sneered, getting closer to my face. "But it really doesn't matter, does it? Because you could be older, or younger, like Ellie and Taryn, it wouldn't make a difference because of who your parents are."

I stopped walking, freezing in place as tears fought for a way to emerge.

"What difference does it make who my parents are? Your mom and mine are best friends; we see each other more than even the other kids do. We've had more sleepovers, more family outings, more vacations. Why are you so mean to me?"

A hiccup nearly had my voice cracking, but I slammed my mouth closed as my body shook with rage. Connor was the nice one, the one who was always kind, always considerate, always making sure Ford wasn't being a jerk.

Snow fell against Ford's lashes, his hazel eyes moved, as if he were searching for something on my face.

"My dad was the president before yours. My grandpa started this club. My mom was raised in it. By rights, it should fall to me, but because your dad runs it, it's not going to stay in the Stone family."

My eyes narrowed in frustration as I shouldered past him, moving closer to the door. "You're not the Stone family. You're the Ryan family, and you're an idiot. My dad was raised by your grandpa, we're practically cousins, you moron."

We were nearly to the door when Ford let out a scoff. "We are not cousins."

I sneered back, "I said practically."

His cheeks flushed red as he shook his head, then pulled open the door to the back of the club. Heat rushed to my face as we made our way into the separate kitchen area, where just a washer and dryer were. The door leading into the main part of the kitchen was closed, so no one saw us enter.

I kicked off my boots and slid out of my jacket; Ford did too.

"Do you think they're okay?" I asked, hoping he would be nice for once with his reply.

He shrugged, then quickly moved to the door, watching through the crack to see if it was clear.

Once it was, we moved silently to the pantry.

The small light flickered on, and then Ford pulled on the cellar door.

"I should have gone with them," Ford murmured from ahead of me. I crossed my arms over my chest to ward off the chill of the cold room. I was in my socks, which felt like nothing at all because of the cold basement floor.

"Well, I needed help pulling the door."

Ford scoffed, but I let it go. He could make fun of me all he wanted, but, deep down, he knew I was right.

We were both at the small wooden hatch, staring down at it. Ford moved to a crouch and began pulling, but the door wouldn't budge.

He glanced at me once, and then pulled again, groaning as he pulled yet again, but nothing happened. Breathing heavily, he sat next to the hatch when suddenly there was knocking from underneath it and a muffled yell from Connor.

"You guys up there?" I managed to make out from Connor yelling.

I rushed to place my mouth down near the door. "We're here!"

Ford was right next to me, our faces merely inches apart. "We can't pull it, can you try shoving your shoulder up against it?"

We were both breathing heavily waiting for Connor to reply.

"Yeah, count to three!"

Ford got to his knees, then gave me a stern look. "I need your help."

I nodded, knowing we couldn't argue about it. "How?"

"Put your hands over mine, and then we pull together."

I waited for him to get his hands in place, and then moved, so mine covered his. It placed us directly next to each other, so close I could feel his breath on my neck. We didn't move, or do anything, so I turned my face to see what he was waiting on.

"Should I count?"

Ford just stared at me, his mouth parted, like he'd been struck dumb. If I wasn't holding the latch with him, I'd wave my hand in front of his face to make sure he was awake.

"Ford, should I count?"

Those hazel eyes searched my face again, and I wished so badly that I knew what he was looking for, just so I could make it stop. Because his look made me feel something warm in my chest, like a hot coal from a fire had been placed there, but it didn't burn, it was just warm and safe.

"Ford?"

He finally blinked then nodded.

I turned my face back toward the door and started counting.

"One."

Ford moved so his face was practically next to mine.

"Two."

I tightened my hand over his to get ready, and I could hear Ford intake a sharp breath.

"Three!" I yelled, heaving my arms up, right as Ford did, but as our arms raised, Ford's mouth was next to my face, and suddenly I felt his lips press into my cheek.

I froze, then heard him whisper, "I wish I could really hate you. It would be easier."

I let go of the handle, mostly out of shock, but Ford took my place, and with another heavy pull, the hatch lifted and Connor's face appeared.

"You're alive!" I smiled at my friends, trying to ignore what had just happened with Ford.

Ford moved back and pulled on my elbow, so they had more space to crawl through. Both Rook and him had dirt smudges on their faces and in their hair.

"So, find anything crazy?" Ford asked, as they both climbed through the tunnel.

Rook let out a heavy sigh as he fell to the floor and stared up at the ceiling.

"Yeah."

I waited for him to finish, but he just kept breathing.

Ford asked, "So, what was down there?"

Connor finally replied, glancing over at Rook like he wasn't sure he should say anything.

"More tunnels."

TWELVE
JAMESON

I finally managed to pull my wife away from the main room and get her alone.

My hands were in her hair, my lips at her neck as I pulled her into my chest, and just breathed. We hadn't had any time to really process what had happened yesterday; even after arriving, we had focused on the kids and catching up with the threat. Even as we laid in bed last night, our kids were in the same room, so it wasn't like I could really process with her. Not in the way I needed to.

"Jamie, what's going on?" Pen whispered in my ear while my mouth was still marking her throat.

My eyes nearly watered as I recalled the way that moment felt, when I saw that rider in the middle of the road with his gun aimed at our truck. How in that brief moment I imagined her being taken from me. How I had to swallow the fear that she might be hurt and just act. All night, I had that moment frozen in my mind, and the terror that lingered of what would have happened to me, or the kids, if she wasn't here anymore.

Even now, it made me physically shake at how helpless it made me feel.

"I just needed a second to hold you…"

Pen leaned away from me while gripping my wrists. "You're shaking, Jameson. You never shake."

I tried to give her a smile, but instead I just pulled her face up and pressed my lips to hers.

We were in the basement, where our little family had been placed, but there was a laundry room with a door that locked. I started walking us backward and toward it when Penelope stopped me, searching my face.

"Talk to me."

Our foreheads pressed together as I let out a shudder. "I can't get it out of my head. The image of him aiming that gun at us. At you. I need to touch you, feel you. Know you're with me."

Her hand came up to stroke my back in a soothing fashion. "I'm always with you."

"Don't say that, baby…please, because all it does is remind me of those funerals we attended where we tried to encourage people grieving that their loved ones are always with them."

She must have understood what I was trying to say, or at least get at because after a few silent seconds, she gripped my hand and walked with me back to the laundry room.

I shut the door and flipped the lock.

She glanced at the washer. "Take what you need, Jamie. Honestly, I need it too. I'm good at shoving it down for the kids, but I'm still seeing it too. Still flashes in my mind when I close my eyes."

Nodding, I started unbuttoning my jeans, and my wife let out a small sigh.

"I don't know how long we'll have."

"It'll be enough," I whispered, moving closer to her. Our lips met, and within seconds, our tongues moved against each other in a caress that silently spoke of our fear. Our trauma. The sliver of safety we lived within, the shadow that seemed to be cast over our lives with every waking breath. And yet, this was the life we wanted to live, our family. Our choice, and we'd never walk away from it.

My wife was in a simple pair of black leggings, with a long-sleeved shirt that gaped at her collarbone, but was long enough to cover her ass. Under it, she wore her favorite bra. I'd never told her it was my favorite of hers too. Not because it was sexy, or anything else but because it was something she loved, and I loved anything that made my wife feel at home in her own body.

I tugged at her leggings, pushing them down, until they were a pool of fabric at her feet. She stepped out of them then looped her arms around my neck.

My hands went to her ass, as I lifted her to the washer.

"Cold." She hissed against my lips.

Shit, I should have thought of bringing in a blanket or something for her. I slid my shirt off and then lifted her, so she was sitting on it. Her hands came up to cradle my jaw as she pressed a gentle kiss to my lips.

"I love you, Jameson King."

Emotion clogged my throat as the events from yesterday flashed through my mind once more. I pushed them away and kissed her back, then replied, "I love you, Penelope King."

Our kisses transitioned from sweet to desperate quickly. She buried her fingers in my hair while mine traced her thighs. Her skin was silky under my touch, and I was completely obsessed with how she tasted. Even ten years later, I was fucked when it came to her. She undid me in every way.

With my hand at her back, I helped her recline, while angling her so that her hips were lifted, and within reach of my mouth. I locked eyes with her as I lowered my face between her legs and began pressing gentle kisses into the sides of her thighs.

"How wet are you for me, Mrs. King?"

She spread her legs for me and brought her hand down to rub circles over her clit. "Taste."

She put her fingers to my mouth, and I cradled her wrist in my hand, then began licking her fingers. My wife watched me with her mouth parted, like she was desperate for whatever I'd do next. After I finished with her fingers, I smiled at her then sank my own digits into her pussy.

"My turn."

My voice was a rasp as I added another finger and began fucking her with them. Her head fell back as I pulled them out, then slowly slid them back in. Once they were glistening with her arousal, I pulled them free and raised my hand to her mouth. She mimicked my move by cradling my wrist and sucking my fingers. She was a sight to behold with her legs spread wide, her shirt lifted, showing her tits being held up by her navy bra. It showed the swells of her breasts in a way that had me staring with hooded eyes.

"I taste like I'm desperate for you to fuck me," she whispered, once my fingers were sucked clean. I pulled my hand back and pulled her ass closer to the edge of the washer before lowering my face to her spread thighs.

Tracing her bare slit with my nose, I inhaled the scent of that desperation. My erection pressed against my jeans, the tip leaking with precum against my boxer briefs, but I didn't care. I just needed to taste my wife and then I'd sink into her.

With my eyes on hers, I gently pried her pussy lips apart and began licking the seam. Slow, measured and with intent to taste every fucking drop of her creamy arousal.

"Jameson." She panted loudly.

The last thing I wanted was for our kids to come down here and hear us fucking. So, I reached my hand forward and turned the dial on the older washer machine then pulled it, so the water would start filling the basin. She did the same with the dryer next to her, moving the dial and pushing in, so it started. The noise filled the room, and now her ass was moving because the dryer was old and shook when it was started.

"That's my girl, now you can moan my name and tell me how much you love me licking this fucking pussy. You can tell me how badly you want me to fuck you. Why don't you show me how badly you need my cock."

She moaned, lifting her hips, while reaching for my hair.

I let her dig her nails into my scalp while she let out her little cries of pleasure and I continued lapping at her cunt. She was spread so wide; I had the perfect angle to press my tongue into the tight hole of her ass. She loved when I added pressure there while fucking her, but she was equally as excited if I added pressure while eating her out.

I added more lubrication to her, then ever so gently added my finger to the tight bundle of nerves. We had anal fairly regularly, but without lube, I had to be cautious of how she felt as I stretched her.

"Let me know if you're good, baby," I muttered before pressing a kiss to her clit, then circling it with my tongue.

She pulled my hair but lifted her hips, which had my finger going deeper.

"You like me licking your pussy while I slowly fuck your ass?"

She made an unintelligible sound, but it was pleasure. Pure fucking pleasure.

I spit again on her hole, ensuring it was lubricated enough while I slowly and gently added a second finger to her ass, stretching her. Then with my tongue, I went back and swiped at her clit, lapping at it in a way that had her moaning.

"Come for me, Pen."

My mouth returned to her pussy, which had her crying out and trying to close her legs around my head.

I lifted my face and stared down at her sex. I used my fingers to swipe the lubrication from her cunt and spread it around her tight hole that was now stretched enough for us to play.

Her chest was still heaving when I pulled up on her long-sleeved shirt to fully remove it. Once it was on the floor with her leggings and thong, I pulled on her hips and brought her to my chest in a hug.

Her breasts pressed against my chest, the soft fabric from her bra sliding against my skin.

She was still trying to catch her breath when I pressed a kiss to her mouth, light and soft, then gave her a feral smile.

"This part might be a little rough, but I promise you'll like it."

Her mouth parted for only a second before I had her slide down my front, and then once her feet were on the floor, I turned her so that she was facing the washer.

"Wha—"

"Place your hands here and hang on," I rasped close to her ear, while placing my hands over hers and guiding them to the edge of the washer, in two places where I wanted her to hold on. Her chest was flat against the closed lid of the machine, and her ass was right where I wanted it. I lightly skimmed the expanse of her cheeks with my hands, then lightly slapped.

Her right leg came up as I gently pulled on it, then I angled it, and had her knee rest on the surface, which exposed her pussy to the air…and to me.

"Keep holding on."

Pen looked over her shoulder, right as I unzipped my jeans and let them slip down past my ass. The band of my boxer briefs was next as I held her leg in place with one hand and gripped my cock in the other.

I lined myself up with Pen's slit, and then holding onto her hips, I thrust. My wife gave a gasp, and I was only half way inside her. Pulling out, I lined up once more, and then gave another hard push, burying myself inside her completely. I froze while Pen adjusted to me. She took me nearly every night, and yet each time, it was like our first, where she had to slowly acclimate to having me inside her.

Within seconds, Pen was looking over her shoulder at me and releasing her hold on the edge to grip her ass cheek, so I had better access to her. I used the freedom to press my thumb into her asshole while I continued to rock into her.

Pen bit her lip while she watched, and she looked so fucking sexy with her dark hair spilling over her back, her pink lip caught in her teeth, and those dark lashes resting against her cheek as her eyes closed.

"Jameson," she whispered in desperation.

My hips canted as I fucked her. The washer and dryer moved, and their sounds filled the room, but my wife's were starting to rival them with her cries of pleasure.

I was practically in a trance as I moved my cock rapidly in and out of her cunt, so tight and wet. My thumb pressed into her hole, adding the pressure I knew she needed. It made her insatiable, rocking her ass into me with such fervor that the washer began to rock more than it was supposed to.

"Fuck," I yelled, grabbing hold of her wrist and keeping it in place as I finished.

Pen cried out, right as I froze with my cock buried so deep in her pussy that I was panting, and my knees nearly gave out.

After I stood there, catching my breath, I pulled out and lowered her leg.

Pen let out a sigh while slowly pushing off from the washer. "Not the most comfortable position we've ever done, but it was hot."

I smirked, and then pressed a kiss to her head while she started pulling her clothes into her arms.

"I'm going to run over to the bathroom real quick and clean up."

I popped my head out to make sure no one was in the room before giving her the green light to go. It would have been nice to use the shower to fuck, but the basement bathroom was small and old. It had a narrow stall, barely tall enough for anyone six foot to stand under.

While Pen cleaned up, I pulled my clothes on and stopped the washer and dryer, feeling slightly guilty that there wasn't anything in either, and we'd just used up all that electricity to silence the sounds of our fucking.

"Jamie?" Pen called for me from the opposite end of the room.

In the middle was the couch and all our bedding, seeing as we'd be staying another night.

"You had to process, and now I need to by asking questions. I have a lot of them."

Penelope was never excluded from club politics, or drama, but I didn't freely offer information either. Sometimes things were just better left unsaid, and not dug into. Some things were better if she didn't know, so in this situation, I could understand it digging under her skin.

"Of course."

She moved to the bedding and started folding blankets while glancing up at me from time to time.

"Is it the Destroyers?"

"As far as we know, yes."

Her chest heaved, and her blue eyes were suddenly sharp as she glared at the clothes Nova had left behind on the floor. The pile Pen had specifically told her to pick up before she got dressed earlier.

"How is that possible?"

I ran a hand through my hair, blowing out a breath. "We haven't figured that part out yet."

"Is it someone who just picked up the reins from Fable?"

She aggressively shook out a pair of jeans from Connor, then tossed them into his duffel bag.

I watched her while I wished for better news to give her.

"We think there might be a familial connection to him…we aren't sure, but we think he may have had another son."

Pen's gaze was locked on mine now. Frozen, as if I'd just grown two heads.

"That's what Laura alluded to as well. But wouldn't it make more sense that one of Fable's brothers took up the vendetta? We always assumed it was possible since the final blame for his death was placed on the Stone Riders."

I was already shaking my head. "They knew it was Silas. Remember four years ago when Silas, Natty and the boys had to leave the country for a while?"

Her shoulders dropped. "Oh yeah."

"So why is everyone assuming it's another son then?"

I still wasn't entirely sure myself, but I'd been listening to what Killian had said.

"Rachel, Killian's mom, talked to him after he called her. She's living in Boston right now, but he called her after Giles talked to him about the threat. Rachel mentioned another son."

Pen's nose flared, and I knew she was pissed. "Why the actual fuck wouldn't she have said something by now about him? Especially after what Silas and Natty went through four years ago with Fable's brothers?"

"Who's to say she didn't talk to them?"

My wife let out a sigh, while angrily making the rest of our bed, fluffing pillows before she calmed down enough to speak again.

"So you think Rachel bypassed Laura and Killian and talked to Silas and Natty herself?"

I gave a slight shrug. "Rachel and Natty have a relationship…so yeah, it's possible they talked and know things that haven't been shared with everyone."

"Well, that's bullshit. I want a little confession time with everyone." Pen tossed the last pillow before pushing her hair back. "Let's go."

I walked forward and lightly grabbed her elbow. "We need Silas here to do that, and it might be better that he isn't here."

"Why is that?"

I searched Pen's eyes, trying to infuse her with some kind of hope. Anything to help push her through this stupid bump in the road. Another fucking bump. Another obstacle in between us being safe and happy. Another problem that needed solving.

"Because Killian is pissed and has a mind to shoot Silas on the spot. Regardless that his wife and kids are here. Frankly, they're the only reason he hasn't made the order yet. But when Silas gets here, there's going to be blood that's shed. Make no doubt about it."

Just then there was a commotion from upstairs, with the sound of feet running, and then we heard the door open above the stairs and someone run down. Connor poked his head down, looking at us both with a concerned expression.

"Silas is here; he's hurt and he's not alone."

THIRTEEN
SILAS

Blood soaked the white snow below my feet.

I would have laughed if it didn't hurt so fucking much, but only because I recalled how Ryle had written in his letter to Santa that he wanted a white Christmas. Then he crossed that out, and wrote that he wanted a white and red Christmas.

Hopefully he wasn't at the door when someone finally registered that we'd pulled up. This was going to be a clusterfuck, but we were out of options, and I wasn't in the mood to deal with any more bullshit. Not after the last twenty-four hours.

"Come on, you assshole. Don't make me carry you." Lance groaned, shifting his weight, so he was helping me walk. I was bleeding out, and while he should have taken me to a hospital, I knew I was going to die there. If not from bleeding out, then from one of The Destroyers finding me and ending me right there in the hospital.

I wouldn't leave this earth without seeing Natty's face first.

Those eyes that knew exactly what I was feeling, her soul would crack and break once I left this earth, but she deserved to at least be with me as it happened.

Coughing, I tried to apply more weight to my step, so Lance didn't have to carry all of it.

"Sorry. Forgot how weak you are. You stopped lifting since you became president, haven't you? Told you…It's important to stay strong, Lance. Especially with that new little—"

I stumbled, and everything went blurry.

I heard Lance yelling, then I looked up toward the front door of the club and there she was.

She was running. Her wild hair flying behind her as she screamed my name. Lance held out his arms to catch her, but she pushed him off. Her voice was shrill, but it still sounded so perfect in my ears.

"Caelum." I held up my hand, hating that it was covered in blood. I wanted to touch her hair, but it was soft and so light. Like starlight.

"Silas, what—" Her voice broke as her fingers came to my jaw, then my chest. She was blurry, but I saw tears falling from her lashes. I loved those lashes. I kissed them when we fucked sometimes because she smiled when I did it, and I loved her smile.

"He was shot while we were riding back. He managed to stay on his bike the whole way here, but once we got through the gates, I saw how bad it was. He can't go to a hospital."

"Why the fuck not?" Natty's voice broke.

I hoped my boys weren't watching. I didn't want them to see this. I didn't mind dying on Stone Riders soil because this was Natty's home, and she was mine.

"Don't cry, Caelum. I love you." I stroked her hair; she was lying on my chest now, crying. That was probably not a good sign if they weren't even trying to help me.

"Not like this, my love. We still have an entire lifetime ahead of us. You promised me years ago, and I'll never forgive you if you leave me, Silas. We have two sons to raise. They need you. Don't you dare stop fighting."

It was hard to speak, my throat hurt, burned and ached as if I'd been yelling. But I managed to whisper, "Numquam."

Never.

Someone else was running toward us, the snow started falling again and I realized I couldn't even feel the cold, but Natty was barefoot, and in just a simple t-shirt. "Give her my coat, Lance. She needs—" I swallowed and tried again, "Take my coat, Caelum. Take my—"

It was hard to talk, and things were getting blurry again as I saw someone else running toward us. They were yelling too…it was the rest of the Stone Riders. They were here to carry me to hell. I smiled one last time at the only heaven I'd ever know, and then I closed my eyes.

FOURTEEN
ROOK

THEY CARRIED HIM IN LIKE HE WAS ALREADY DEAD.

Maybe he was.

Blood soaked his coat, his leather one that still had the Grim Reaper on the back from the club he used to be in. The one Mom said he still loved and considered himself a part of.

Uncle Lance was here too; he had blood all over his coat as well, and he was crying.

I had never seen him cry.

Aunt Callie was too, so was Aunt Laura and then Aunt Penelope was holding Mom really tight.

Mom was shaking. Shaking so hard, I thought she might fall down or be sick. She had blood smeared all over her Frosty the Snowman shirt. Ryle and I had bought it for her last winter; Dad was in the store with us when we found it. We liked it because Frosty had a skull mask on.

Now, there was blood smeared all over it.

Something in my chest felt like it was cracking, but I wasn't sure how to process what it was. Ryle was watching too, but Connor and Royce were sitting between him, holding his hands tight, like they could prevent him from breaking.

Rudolph pranced around with a red light on his nose on the television screen, happy and bright. The Christmas tree had lights on it, and we'd even baked Christmas cookies.

It was a happy day.

Now it wasn't.

I needed to know if my dad was okay, but they were in the kitchen, and my dad was on the counter while two of the older members, Harris, and Pops, began inspecting where my dad was bleeding.

I glanced over at my mom. She wasn't allowed in the kitchen. Aunt Penny held her while they rocked back and forth on the floor and Mom sobbed into the floor, praying that Dad would be spared.

That breaking feeling kept happening. It was cracking and cracking.

I couldn't breathe. My dad went pale, and I saw his fingers limp on the side of the counter. Harris started yelling, and then Pops had another member come in with tubes, and then I was being pulled away.

A warm hand wrapped around mine, and we started moving. We moved so fast I couldn't even see where we were walking until the cellar door was being opened, and we were moving down the stairs. I saw dark hair flying and then I was being pulled to the floor.

"Mommy once told me that she prayed so hard for something that she fell to her knees in the quietest place she could find and she prayed. She didn't stop until she fell asleep. She said God can hear us, sometimes at least. If there's a chance, then we have to take it."

Nova pulled me down until my knees were touching hers.

"You're going to be okay, Rook. It's Christmas, and miracles happen on Christmas. This is the only one we'll ask for, okay?"

I nodded, unable to speak. I watched as Nova closed her eyes and held my hand in hers, and then she began to pray.

"Save him. Please God, save Uncle Silas."

She didn't stop, she just kept saying it over and over and over again. The same words on repeat. It was soothing in a way because it took away the breaking feeling to the point where all I did was repeat what she was saying.

"Save him," I said, and Nova still didn't look up. "Please God, save my dad."

I watched her lips move. Watched as tears slipped past her lashes, and I watched as her heart tried to grow legs, to walk the space between us, and to settle near mine. She was trying to help me. To comfort me.

It stitched back together something. I wasn't sure what it was, but it felt warm and right.

I just kept watching her until we were both getting so tired, we laid down on the rug. I knew there was a hatch door under us because I'd walked through it earlier.

Part of me wanted to open it again and let it swallow me.

"Rook, if your heart breaks, don't worry. I'll give you mine."

I didn't cry. No tears would come, but I reached for her hand while I stared at the ceiling.

"Make sure it doesn't stop beating, Nova. Because it feels like it might stop…it feels frozen."

I could feel Nova turn her head toward me. "I'll protect it, Rook. Just sleep. When you wake up, you'll have your miracle. Just wait and see."

FIFTEEN
NATTY

Penelope brushed my hair back while soothing me with her words. Callie and Laura were with my kids somewhere…at least I hoped they were. But my mind was blank.

Blank and yet painfully full of every memory, every flashback. Every piece of history I had with Silas.

Back to bullfrogs on summer days on our dock.

To the moment our sons were born, and the way Silas smiled that first time with each of them. How he read to them at night and sang silly songs in the morning. How he loved me.

Perfectly, and fully…he loved me the way sonnets were written. The way rain fell, and sunsets painted the skies. Silas loved me like I was his universe, and in turn, I lived as though he were mine. Without him, I couldn't—

Another sob came unbidden from my chest. I couldn't control them. Tears ran freely, and even if I wanted to put on a brave face for my kids, I wouldn't be able to. It was Christmas Eve, and we were spending it losing Silas.

Silas. My husband. My life.

"She needs water," Penelope said to someone.

"She's going to need something stronger than water, Pen." That was Jameson.

I blinked, and more tears trailed down my face.

"Don't doubt me, young Jameson King. I have saved many a man from rival wars. I was a field medic in the war," Pops said happily.

He was old. Too old to likely see the way he needed to see. Silas had lost too much blood, even if there was a transfusion with one of the other members who had stepped up and offered, I wasn't sure it would be enough and I was too terrified to hope. I couldn't lose him.

I couldn't.

I wouldn't make it.

"We need to get her out of here." That was Wes, sounding fearful or worried.

Fuck him. I wasn't moving. In fact, all I wanted was to go lie next to my husband while he lay dead on the counter that I had spent so much time baking away my worries. Baking more time into my life while I waited for him.

So much of our life was spent waiting on each other, and these last ten years didn't come close to making up for it. I wanted more.

I demanded more.

Suddenly I got to my knees, pushing Penelope's hands off of me, and I stomped into the kitchen, seeing them place new bandages over my husband's gunshot wound.

"Silas!" I screamed.

Pops looked over, and I waited for the pity to come, but he didn't give it. Neither did Harris.

"He has to fight." I hiccupped. I knew I looked crazy, but I didn't care. My mascara had run, my face was blotchy and red, my shirt had blood all over it. My husband's blood.

A fire erupted in my stomach with fear. With anguish.

"He has to fight!" I cried, going closer to him.

A gentle hand landed on my shoulder, and someone said close to my ear, "he did, Darlin. He did."

Harrison locked eyes with me, and then gave me a nod. "We've done all we can, but we need to leave the rest up to God."

They both walked out while Killian and Wes came in to grab Silas and gently carry him to a room that had been made up in Laura's office. A twin bed was there with fresh sheets and a pristine pillow.

Silas's shirt was gone. I stared at the inked word over his heart.

Caelum.

My knees gave out as they lay my husband down. He was too pale.

Whatever they had done, it wasn't going to be enough. I felt it.

"We have to get him to the hospital. He needs someone watching his vitals all night."

Killian appeared next to me; his brows creased in worry.

My voice broke as I faced him. "Please, Killian. Please."

His green eyes lifted, like he was the one pleading with me. His jaw clenched, and with one look at Silas, he closed his eyes. "They're watching the hospitals. Silas would want you and the boys to stay safe here. Please understand that. They got the bullet out. There wasn't as much damage as we all assumed. They think he's going to pull through because he's too fucking stubborn not to. Give him the benefit of the doubt, Natty."

I could barely see through the stream of tears that continued to flow. Swiping at my face, I tried to think through another option. Any other option.

"What about Archer Green?"

Killian's brow raised. "Archer?"

"We made an alliance with Archer a long time ago, and even if he's mostly retired, I know he'll honor it. We have Giles, and now we have Lance."

I was desperate. I could feel it, but down in my bones I knew he would not last the night.

"What exactly are you proposing we do? Archer Green hasn't set foot outside of New York aside from visiting his wife's family, but that's an entirely different shitshow that I want nothing to do with…involving him with his new connections would be even more dangerous because we don't know which side he'd fall on. Regardless, we can't even move Silas, Natty."

I knew that, yet my heart demanded we try.

"What if we can bring a doctor to him with supplies? Everything he'd need."

A sigh left Killian's chest, but with one small flick of his gaze, he was staring behind me. I could feel my sons' presence, and while everything inside of me felt brittle to the point of breaking completely in half, I continued to stare at Killian.

Let him see my son stand there. Let him watch as he refused to do absolutely everything within his power to save my husband.

"What would you do if it were Laura?" I stepped closer, still swiping as tears filled my eyes. My voice cracked, but I kept going.

"You would do everything, and I would help you do it."

His gaze was still on my son, his nostrils flaring wide as he seemed to think it through.

"I'll make a call and see if we can get one here. Pen seemed to know one who helped us a long time ago…maybe she's still around."

I turned with him, seeing Ryle standing there, wide eyes and trembling lip.

"I don't care who it is, Killian. Archer has men close to Rose Ridge. Call him to go with you, help you. The Death Raiders will ride with you. Giles will go with you. Find a doctor, I don't care who or if they want to come. Ask what they'll need to keep my husband alive through the night."

Killian shook his head, "It's Christmas Eve—"

"The alternative, Killian," I cut him off, stepping up to him, my anger surging, "is that I take Lance with me, and I ride myself to do this. If that happens, I will cut all ties to this club. I will convince Penelope to have Jameson return to the Chaos Kings and I promise you, Lance will have my back as we take up the colors of the Death Raiders again. I have stood by this club as everyone turned their backs on us. Silas has rode with you, protected you. But if you don't do this, I will do it and that is your choice."

Lance suddenly stepped into the room, standing directly behind me. "If you decide to help, I'll make an alliance with you right now. Death Raiders will have your back no matter what, we'll be indebted to you for life."

Killian's face didn't change even the slightest bit, but his fists clenched nearly as tightly as his jaw.

"And if he doesn't make it?"

Lance spoke again, his own voice cracking the smallest bit. "He is my brother. My family. Try, that's all we're asking. Try and you have my support for life, whether he makes it or not."

"This is a fucking suicide mission. We don't have the numbers; even if I wanted to ask Archer, he could never get his men here in time. What you're asking of me, you need to put in writing, so the club has your vow, Lance. So whoever leads after me…they'll have Death Raider support no matter what."

Killian pushed past us, clearly upset but agreeing, nonetheless.

Lance put a hand on my shoulder and squeezed. "Don't lose heart, Natty. Give all you've got to him, and more. He calls you heaven. Let's see if you hold any sway with it while we beg for him to be spared."

SIXTEEN
KILLIAN

THIS WAS A DEATH SENTENCE.

I knew from the scouts that kept texting me that the roads weren't safe, and the Destroyers were everywhere. We didn't have bulletproof vehicles, and most of us just rode our bikes, regardless of the danger.

But it was snowing and the roads were icy. There was also the little issue of taking a doctor hostage and hauling back all the shit they needed.

"Let me lead the group. I'll create a diversion. Or put me in charge of grabbing the doc," Giles offered while sliding his gun into the back waist of his jeans.

I glanced over at Wes, who had his head down and his jaw locked. I knew what thoughts were running through his head. I knew how hard this was for him and Callie. It was Christmas Eve, and the club wasn't supposed to interfere with family time. It was a rule we lived by, but there was nothing we could do. Nothing to be done, because if Natty lost Silas, the damn holiday would be ruined. I had never grown a single fuck for the guy, even after ten years. But I cared about Natty, Rook and Ryle.

I cared about the way Laura hugged me so tight I thought my chest might break, and how she whispered thank you to me. How she promised that she'd see me later, and that this wouldn't be our end. The way I held onto her words was the only thing that had me moving.

"Giles, if you want Chaos Kings to lead, then fine, but I was thinking of having Death Raiders lead, and Chaos Kings follow."

Jameson glanced over at me and gave a small nod.

As a previous president, his opinion mattered, and every now and then he'd silently give me a nod, just to encourage me that he agreed with what I was doing. It was a small mercy.

Lance stepped up, a phone to his ear. "Death Raiders can lead. They're waiting on my call."

I gave a small nod, still fighting this feeling in my gut. We'd been in battle plenty of times, but each time I left feeling like we'd come home at the end. This was the first time I left mounting my bike while knowing there was a good chance this would be the last time I saw my family.

Holding my helmet in my hands, my leather jacket had slid up, revealing my wrist. I tilted it forward to see the three daisies I had tattooed there.

Laura, Royce and Taryn.

My three reasons for living. With one last look at the club, I secured the strap of my helmet under my chin and started my bike, then I ignored the two blonde-haired little girls crying while they watched me ride away.

SEVENTEEN
WES

"I have the doctor, but how the fuck are we supposed to get out of here?" Giles asked through the speaker on my phone.

We were tucked inside a building, lying low after riding for our lives to get here. Two of Giles' men were shot, and possibly more of the Death Raiders. I hadn't even seen how many Stone Riders had pulled in after us.

The second we got on the road, we were surrounded. The Destroyers were waiting for us, and we barely got away with our lives just getting here.

Killian was staring at the phone in my hand, and I was staring back at him, but my mind was on a pair of hazel eyes that I'd known since childhood. Callie's smile and the way the sun always cut through her hair when we sat outside, watching our kids play. How she'd pull Ellie's hair back and they'd both look in the mirror and giggle because of how similar they looked.

How she'd worry about Ford, but never show him.

She was the best thing that ever happened to me and we'd cheated death so many times in our lives, perhaps this was it. The final time, and maybe Death was being merciful by not taking her or my kids, and instead was only coming for me.

Giles coughed, then replied to our silence, "Do either of you have any ideas? The Destroyers have us surrounded."

I had nothing. I knew Killian didn't either, but he was likely going to tell us to just ride as far as we could.

"Giles, get the doc in their own car. Make sure you're not seen when you get in with them. Have them drive through the woods to get to the entrance C on the property. Get the doctor to the club, no matter what. Your club will divert them by joining with us as we group together and ride back. No one will be with us, but they'll assume there is based off our formation."

Thank fuck for our president being able to think in shitty situations like this. My gut was flipped, my nerves shot, and all I wanted to do was crawl into bed with my wife.

Giles came back on before he hung up. "They've got the numbers, Kil."

Killian refused to acknowledge that, and instead hung up the phone.

It was time to move.

Giles got out using Killian's tactics.

We made sure he wasn't followed, then started our own journey back.

Darkness covered us as we rode like hell down the highway. The blizzard that had hit our town the night prior still lingered, making the road conditions abysmal. By all rights, we were fucking crazy for riding, but there was an odd safety we felt being on two wheels and being able to stay together. Our bikes were so close that one wrong move, and we'd wreck, but the boys all knew the drill. It needed to look like we were hiding someone. So we rode.

I removed my leather cut because if I was found dead, I'd want Callie to know that I died a free man. Her man. My wedding ring would be the only brand I had that tied us together. I wanted her to know that in death, I'd still choose her over the club. Any day, any time. If we could go back in time, I'd refuse the patch, but maybe that wouldn't have mattered. Maybe Callie and I were destined to live those seven years apart, and my heart was meant to go through the loss.

Regardless, if this ride were to be my last, then it would be in honor of her.

The echo of engines roared around me as we traveled under moonlight. Snow swirled above us, and the eerie glow of outdoor Christmas lights illuminated the incoming fog as we passed home after home. I refused to hope that we'd make it out alive.

Not when I knew the Destroyers were watching, and likely just waiting for us to get close to the club.

We were a mile out, and that's when we saw them.

An entire line of headlights flicked on, blocking the road, making it impossible to pass. Giles's crew was in front, and their headlights shone, revealing the row of men in front of the bikes, all leveling shotguns at us.

The Chaos Kings were going to die first.

We would need to stop if we had a fighting chance. Our bikes would get shot to hell, but we'd be able to pull out our own guns and fire back.

I started slowing, which made the group behind me slow, and that's when I saw Killian swing his gaze toward me, as if he wasn't sure what I was doing.

He started slowing as well, but we were too late. Gunfire rang out, which made the front of the line lie down their bikes, sliding along the pavement. Everyone else veered off course to avoid the wreck, and the gunfire, but it wasn't our guys getting shot.

My leg came out to help keep my bike up as I moved to the side with the group, but I was watching the Destroyers, as each and every one of them went down. Someone was shooting them.

I searched the area, but couldn't see anyone…until a fleet of headlights came into view, approaching from behind the Destroyers.

Killian was next to me, his gun drawn. "Who the fuck is that?"

EIGHTEEN
ARCHER GREEN
TWO DAYS EARLIER

Rage wasn't something I felt often, at least not anymore.

People around here knew what the patch on my back meant. When Mayhem Riot was mentioned, eyes would drop, and people would usually get the fuck out of dodge. But that was a long time ago…we rode mostly for fun these days. Not much was running through our club, not since my wife's family made their position clear on who owned this city.

I'd be a fucking moron to enter into a turf war with them, so we ride for fun. We act as muscle when needed, but rarely does dust get kicked up. Especially in the winter, when Christmas was merely a few days away.

Today, I felt rage.

I felt it so strongly that the casing around my heart, and all the darkness in my soul, threatened to leak out and smother every move I made and every word I spoke.

"To be clear, you're making a threat?" I asked, staring directly at the man in front of me.

The man in the middle, he was the leader. He didn't say he was, and he wore no patches indicating as such, but he had a presence about him that made my skin crawl. It was the gut check you got before something bad was about to happen. It's what I felt the second he walked into my club.

He had dark hair and dead eyes. Eerily similar to another man I knew.

Sitting back in his chair, surrounded by his men, made him untouchable. In his left hand, he held something, but I couldn't make out what it was. In his right was nothing but a dark ink stain of some symbol. It was faded, so much so I couldn't make it out.

"At the risk of sounding sardonic, I don't make threats. I merely deliver you a headline of what's to come. So if you'd like to be aware and change course, then you can."

His voice was clear and without emotion; his pale skin was marred with a long scar along his cheek and eyebrow, and all along the back of his hands.

"What club are you a part of?" I flicked my gaze over his men's patches, but none of them were wearing anything that tied them to an affiliation.

The leader tipped his head and let out a small sigh.

"When it's needed, I'll inform you."

My vice president glared at me, silently telling me not to do anything stupid. The men behind me were likely all thinking the same thing. There was something sinister about this man in front of me, and I wasn't stupid enough to ignore that.

I was, however, not smart enough to remove my wedding ring prior to this little meeting, which is why my rage was simmering.

"So, if I agree to go to war with you against the Stone Riders, you'll ensure my wife doesn't befall any mishaps?"

The leader inclined his head.

"Heard she's awfully clumsy in heels."

Mother. *Fucker*.

My fists clenched tightly under the table as my vice president shifted beside me. My men moved forward, forcing his men to raise their weapons.

"She's pretty too, right? I heard that…haven't seen any pictures yet, but I was thinking I might go see her in person. That might be a fun little project for me. Just watch her move."

I was going to fucking kill him.

But it was very likely that I wouldn't even get the chance. Fucking idiot obviously hadn't looked into who my wife's family was. I'd let that get back to him at the least inconvenient time as humanly possible. As it was, my security footage was being shared with her brother as we spoke.

Whoever this man was, was completely fucked, but he didn't need to know that yet.

I forced a smile and stood up.

"You got yourself a deal. We'll help you go to war against the Stone Riders. Never much liked those fuckers anyway."

NINETEEN
FORD

ANOTHER TEAR SLID DOWN THE SIDE OF ROYCE'S FACE.

She didn't know I was watching her sleep, or try to sleep. Our dads were all gone, out on the run to try and find a doctor for Uncle Silas. Our moms were in with Aunt Natty, holding her while she tried not to lose it. Rook and Ryle were in here with us, awake. I knew they were awake because we were all feeling the same thing tonight.

Which was why I was watching the salty tear drop roll down Royce Quinn's face.

We were scared.

The Christmas tree was lit, glowing in the corner with the few decorations we managed to find. Fire still crackled in the hearth, and with all of our blankets, we were cozy. We'd pulled all the cushions off the big sectional and made a huge mattress on the floor, then covered it in blankets and pillows.

It was Christmas Eve, and while we'd tried all day to go with the flow and be happy, we were all finally letting our emotions out. Our fears and worries.

All I really wanted to do though was wipe that tear off Royce's cheek and then hug her so tight, she didn't shed anymore. Her dad was out there, but so was mine. We were both scared, so I wasn't even sure what to say to encourage her.

So I just watched her cry, committing each and every tear to memory. It was a new form of torture, but I'd been a jerk to her so I deserved it. I just continued to remind myself that each time my heart felt that little punch, the tug and pull to fix it, that it was a punishment for always being so mean. She'd never know the reason I was mean, or why it would be impossible for me to ever really be nice. My mouth still tingled from kissing her cheek earlier…she never said anything about it, and I hoped she never would. Royce Quinn would end up with Connor, that's just how it was going to be. Connor said so when he was like five, and ever since then he'd been warning me away from her, even if he hadn't come right out and said it.

I didn't mind though. I liked to admire her from afar, but I was also angry with her and how her father had inherited the club when it wasn't his to have. Still, I shouldn't put that on Royce; it wasn't her fault and I knew how badly she worried.

But it had to be okay, it was Christmas.

Bad things didn't happen during such a happy time of year.

The idea sparked something in my mind. A memory my mom had shared about something my grandpa used to do with her. I sat up and threw the blankets off my legs, then carefully maneuvered toward the church where my dad always disappeared for meetings with the other members of the club. Mom had decided to set up our crafting station in there today.

I flipped on the light and shut the door, then started dumping the popsicle sticks and cotton balls out of the glass jars out on the table. There were only a few jars, but it would have to do. Once they were empty, I started pouring various containers of glitter into the jars. There was a red jar, a green jar, blue and gold.

There was only enough to fill each one halfway, and once the lid was secured, I walked back to the room, seeing all the kids sitting up in their spot, waiting for me to return.

"What is that?" Nova asked, swiping the hair out of her face.

Ellie was next to her, and when she caught sight of what I had, she perked up. "Did you make the wish jars like Mommy used to make with Grandpa?"

I nodded, rounding the couch and handing a jar to one kid from each of the four families. Rook took one, Connor took one, then Taryn and lastly, Ellie held the one for our family.

"My mom said she'd make these jars with my grandpa when she was a kid. In this very club, and when she'd make her wish, she'd bury the jar outside. Since we're all waiting on a miracle to bring our dad's back. I figured we could all go bury a jar outside."

Royce stood up and held her hand out to her sister. Their golden hair was braided back, their warm pajamas were holiday themed with snowflakes. I missed the ones she wore with unicorns on them. I watched Royce's gaze lift to mine, then hold there for a second.

"Let's go wish for our miracle before Santa comes."

All the kids got up, moving together as we quietly moved to the back where our boots were. Then once we were all wearing our gear, we slipped outside, holding the jars.

A large, full moon shone overhead, casting light over the white snow that crunched under our boots as we walked. Our breaths clouded in front of us, but there was something about being outside on Christmas Eve in the dark, under the pale moon that felt magical.

"How are we supposed to dig? The ground is frozen," Rook asked, kicking his boot through the snow.

I hadn't thought of that.

Staring down at the snow, I felt my face flush until Royce bent down, pushing her knees into the snow and cradling her jar.

"We can bury it in the snow. Maybe that's the only way it would work on Christmas Eve, anyway. Maybe this is how we access the magic."

Taryn joined her in the snow, both of their pajamas would be ruined now. Then Rook followed suit with Ryle and Ellie. Then Connor and Nova, until we were all in a circle. I was the last to kneel in the snow, but once I was on the ground, we all started gently pushing the snow away, so a small crater formed.

"What do we say?" Taryn asked, staring down at her gold glitter.

My sister, Ellie, answered, gently taking our jar. "We wish for our dads to come home safe. We wish for Uncle Silas to wake up."

Everyone looked over at Rook and Ryle, who both had pained expressions. Their pale eyes were even lighter under the moonlight, but their dark hair made them look like something from a story book. Raven's feathers and skin that didn't even seem real.

"We wish for our dads to come home," Royce said.

Nova added the rest, placing their jar into the snow, "And for Uncle Silas to wake up."

We all carefully moved the upturned snow over the crater to bury the jars, and then as we sat there staring at the snow, feeling like maybe what we did was foolish or stupid, it started to snow.

Our faces tipped up, watching the sky as if we were experiencing real magic.

Then we heard it. The sound of a truck driving toward us. None of us moved, but our moms began pouring outside, moving in front of us, as if they knew we'd been outside the entire time.

The truck came to a stop, and Giles quickly opened the door, jumping out with a bag of supplies. The man in the passenger side opened his door and quickly moved toward us, wearing a set of doctor scrubs.

"Who is that?" Ellie asked, whispering next to me.

We stood, watching their every move as I slowly replied.

"That's the doctor who's going to save Uncle Silas."

TWENTY
KILLIAN

The men on the ground were being collected by the Death Raiders in someone's truck.

We were working quickly, but we'd also put in a call to our contact with the police to stay away from this area for a while, so we could clear out.

The Destroyers were gone. One second they were there, with guns aimed at us, and the next, they were going down, one by one, until enough of them realized what was going on and took off. Our men were safe, same with Chaos Kings, and Death Raiders…but the surprise twist in this was the arrival of Mayhem Riot.

"Sorry we were late." Archer Green walked over from where he'd parked his bike.

I was still in shock that he'd just saved our asses.

I extended my hand and shook his, trying to communicate my gratitude. "Can't believe you showed up. I didn't even ask you because I heard you had retired."

He dipped his head, showing the top of his darker blond hair. It was still cut so it hit his collarbone, but it was tied back at his neck, revealing his wide jaw.

"A man that looked like he could be Silas Silva's brother showed up in my club a few days ago, threatening my wife if I didn't go to war with you."

"I take it that didn't sit well with you?"

He let out a laugh, shaking his head. "Not even a little bit."

"And your wife and kids, they safe?"

A devious smile stretched across his mouth, which his hand came up to cover. "They're more than safe. The fucker has no idea who my wife is related to. If he took two seconds to look into my family, he'd realize we had a giant, 'don't fuck with these ones,' sign on our backs."

I remember being surprised back when he'd gotten married and who attended his wedding. Laura and I had been given an invite, as a show of peace after Simon's funeral, and we weren't sure the surrounding clubs' supposed treaty was genuine. Archer got married not long after that, and if I was correct then his wife was connected to—

"Killian!" Jameson called for me with his phone to his ear.

I gave Archer one last nod of thanks and walked away. "What's wrong?"

Jameson said something to the person on the phone, then addressed me. "Giles is at the club with the doctor, but Yeti just spotted two Destroyers riding along our property fence line. We need to get back to the club. Now."

TWENTY-ONE
ROOK

The doctor was in the room with my mom and Aunt Penelope, working on my dad. I wanted to feel hopeful, but I could still hear my mom crying. It was too painful to be in there with them, and Nova was finally asleep. Just like the other kids, so I didn't want to make any noise by turning on the television.

Instead, I decided to go back down to the cellar.

There was something about lying on that rug with Nova that felt like hope. The way she prayed over and over again for my dad to be okay. I felt like that rug was magic now. Some kind of magic at least…for some reason I just wanted to be near it. To continue to feed it hope, and somehow get my dad back.

I flipped the light, pulled up the hatch and slowly made my way down the stairs. The wind from the sliver of space in the old door still whistled, and it was freezing, but I didn't care. The cold was a reminder to stay awake and hope for miracles.

It was almost Christmas. So whatever magic was left in the world would leave soon. I had to somehow grab it, hold it and save it for my dad. By the time I reached the small rug, I was on the verge of tears, but everything in my mind seemed to stop. Because sitting there on my rug was a man I'd never seen before, and the hatch to the tunnel was open.

"Who—Who are you?" My voice cracked as I tried not to let my fear show. The man swung his face in my direction, and I froze again. For an entirely different reason.

"You look like me."

The man's eyes widened as if I surprised him. Then he smiled.

"Well, I think we might be family, little man." He stepped away from the hatch and dusted off his jeans. He had on a thick hoodie that had some faded graphic on it, but it hid his arms, not his hands though. Those were scarred but had tons of ink marking all the available skin.

"You're related to my dad?" I tipped my head back. He looked like my dad, but he looked like me even more.

He knelt down in front of me, getting at my eye level. He had eyes that matched mine. His dark hair was longer too, and a few pieces of silver showed at the roots.

"I'm his brother."

Dad's brother died. "Uncle Alec?"

The man looked surprised for a second but masked it quickly. "Nope."

Dad had never mentioned another brother, neither had Mom. Maybe this was a bad man, or maybe he wasn't supposed to be here…but how did he look like me then?

"Then what's your name?"

He gave me a look that was a little confusing. He wasn't smiling, but he wasn't angry either. He just seemed like he was trying to piece something together. "I'm Max."

"No one has ever mentioned you."

My dad's brother rubbed his chin as if he were contemplating my answer, then he moved to a box sitting on the floor and began digging through it. "No one ever mentioned me? I'm the oldest, how could they not mention me. Are you the oldest, Rook? Could you imagine someone not mentioning you some day?"

I shook my head then wondered if my uncle knew that my dad was upstairs fighting for his life.

"You should know my dad might not make it." My voice was sad, and as much as I tried to mask my pain, it seemed to be leaking through and there wasn't anything I could seem to do about it.

Max seemed to focus on my words, like I'd said something that interested him.

"He was shot?"

I nodded, my throat feeling tight.

Max let out a sigh, then ruffled my hair while he moved to another box, like he was searching for something. "Shit. That wasn't supposed to happen. He upstairs?"

"Yeah, a doctor is helping him."

The expression on Max's face seemed to shift as he moved to the side, taking a seat on the bench.

"Is your dad good to you?"

I moved to sit next to him too. "He's the best."

Max laughed, making his shoulders shake a bit.

"And how about your mom, is she good to you?"

"Yeah, she is."

"Is she the one who told you about your Uncle Alec?"

How did he know that? I tilted my head to check his expression. "Yeah, how did you know?"

His fingers tapped against his knee. "Just a thought."

"How old are you, Rook?"

"Nine."

Max stretched his legs out, leaning against the shelf. "You give much thought to what you'll do once you get old enough?"

I shrugged. "Probably work the orchard, like my dad."

Max seemed to think it over, then he pulled out a pen from his pocket and a piece of paper, and wrote something down. From where I was sitting, I couldn't see it. But once he was finished, he folded it up tight and turned toward me.

"I need you to give this to your dad when he's awake enough to understand."

I carefully took the note and started to open it, but Max put his hand over mine.

"Only your dad."

"But what if he doesn't—"

Max shook his head and held firmer to my hand. "He will."

Just then I heard my mom calling for me from the top of the cellar. I turned to look in that direction, but by the time I turned back around, I saw Max moving back toward the hatch.

"Wait, where are you going? Don't you want to see my dad?"

Max gave me a quick wave, before shaking his head. "Not this time, but be sure he gets that note. Okay?"

He lifted the hatch and started climbing down into the tunnel, and before I could say anything else, he'd closed it and disappeared from view.

TWENTY-TWO
NATTY

Forcing Killian to go find a doctor was the right call.

Dr. Henard worked tirelessly to ensure Silas had a fighting chance, and after a harrowing night, we were in the clear. Giles drove the doc home and told us to take Silas back in for recovery care as soon as we felt it was safe.

Now, it was Christmas morning and my heart was full.

I walked into the living room, seeing bodies strewn about all along the floor, and even some on the couches sans the cushions. Jameson held Penelope to his chest in the corner of one of the couches with a few pillows under their bodies. Killian was passed out in a chair with Laura curled up on his lap, resting under his chin, and Wes was holding Callie on the floor where the kids were, Ford and Ellie tucked right next to them.

We were safe.

All of us, we'd made it again, and as tears gathered in my eyes, I tipped my head back and looked up to see the sun shining through the top of the windows. I knew Simon was watching us, maybe Red and Brooks too. They were all watching us go from one war to another and continue to survive it as a family.

"Mom?" Rook's hand found mine from where he was resting on the floor. I squeezed and then used my other hand to swipe at my tears.

"Hey, are you okay?"

Rook smiled up at me, but he was exhausted, I could tell. I'd found him down in the cellar the night prior, well past midnight. I had no idea what he was doing, but when he'd walked back up those stairs, my son had acted as if he'd seen a ghost.

"Yeah, I'm okay. Is Dad awake yet?"

"He might be, wanna go check?"

Rook gave me a silent nod while clamoring to his feet. We walked into the room together and watched as Silas began to stir. Those eyes that I loved so much cracked open the smallest bit, his pale skin looked as if he'd gotten some color back, but he winced as soon as he shifted to see us better.

Rook moved first, to go to his dad's side, and I was right behind him. I wanted to go get Ryle, but I worried it would wake everyone, and I was selfish. I wanted a few seconds where it was just our family, and ours alone.

"Hey, buddy. Merry Christmas." My husband's voice was practically a whisper, so I turned and grabbed him a cup of water, and made sure the straw was easy access for him to drink. Once he'd taken a few sips, he smiled up at me.

It was the smile that took me back to when we were kids. Back to Latin lessons, hunting for frogs, and watching the sunset on our dock. My heart felt like it had grown in size; somehow, I fell harder for Silas, in every way I assumed I'd loved him with every ounce of love available to my human heart, he'd just taken me deeper.

I leaned down and pressed a kiss to his mouth, covering that smile and breathing in the sweet breath he shuddered against my lips. He was alive.

He was okay.

He was going to make it.

Tears clung to my lashes as Rook spoke to his dad, but I wasn't really listening, or processing, as I thanked whoever was listening for giving me my husband back on Christmas morning.

Silas reached for my hand, and while Rook spoke about what the kids found in the tunnels, and how they buried jars full of magic glitter, my husband held on to me. His arms didn't need to be around me, nor his mouth on me. I just needed his touch; I needed his skin on mine.

Ryle walked in moments later, rubbing the sleep out of his eyes. His dark hair was shifted in all different directions, but his little eyes tracked up, seeing Silas awake and his little smile lit up the whole room. I pulled him into my arms and held him in my lap, so he didn't crawl onto Silas at all. Rook sat close to his father on the other side, and the four of us spent Christmas morning surrounding the greatest gift we could have ever been given.

TWENTY-THREE
CALLIE

We were finally given the green light to leave, but we all felt reluctant to pull away after everything that had happened.

Not to mention, when it was time to move Silas, we'd have to call an ambulance to do it. And we all knew he needed a few more minutes of Christmas with all of us before he went. So, we rolled his bed out into the main foyer of the club, near the fireplace, so we could all be near the tree.

Pen's family was on one side, Laura and Killian were with the girls on another. Silas, Natty and the boys all remained close to the fireplace, and Wes was sitting next to me, while holding Ellie in his lap, and Ford was on the floor near my feet. We were spending Christmas morning together as a club.

As a family.

"This is going to seem really corny, but I feel like we should sing a Christmas song or something," I suggested, feeling my face warm.

Laura immediately stood up, smiling.

"Yes! Okay, I'm going to grab the piano I leave here sometimes for the girls to play on and we're going to sing!" She ran out of the room, toward her office, and then reemerged with a keyboard she set down on the coffee table.

Within seconds, the melody for "Jingle Bells" filled the air, and I couldn't hold back my smile. Ellie and Nova joined with Laura's beautiful voice, nearly eclipsing her, which made everyone laugh. Then the whole room was joining in, and there was something so perfect about us singing it together, it made me think back to when I was a little kid, spending Christmas here, in a much different version of the club. Killian was there for some of those Christmases, so was Red and Brooks. Dad never really knew what to do to make our Christmases nice, so Red would go above and beyond to make it special for me.

I wish he was here now, to see all of us after lasting through the night.

I wish he could see the way Ford watched when his father taught him about bikes. I wish I could hear his thoughts on how Ellie looked like a miniature version of me. But more so, I wanted him to see what sort of leader Killian turned out to be, and how loyal Jameson and Giles ended up being. I wanted him to see Silas still here, being loyal to the Stone Riders when he still clearly preferred the Death Raiders.

My father created something beautiful, and he left before he was even really able to see what it had become.

Laura started a new melody, of "O Christmas Tree," which had Penelope getting up and helping as Connor began pulling out small, wrapped gifts from the tree. Ford jumped up and started helping too. Together, they handed all the adults one gift each.

The wrapping was obviously done by one of the kids, but I held it close to my chest like it was treasure, just like every other adult seemed to do.

"Okay, Connor, you said you and the kids made gifts. What do you mean?" Penelope asked, holding her present like she wasn't sure where to start unwrapping it.

"We made you gifts so your Christmas was happy since Christmas Eve was so scary for everyone," Nova explained, smiling at her mother.

Laura glanced over at me and I knew what she was thinking because we'd given each other that look a thousand times.

These kids were the gift.

Always had been.

"Open them!" Ellie urged everyone. Wes started opening his, and he smiled down at a picture that had been drawn in colored pencil.

Ellie leaned into her father's side, her hands on his leg as she stared down at the picture.

"It's a river because you always call mommy that. But I put me and Ford on the bank, right here." She pointed at the dirt on the side of the river. "Mommy is in the water because she's the river."

Wes looked over at me with tears in his eyes and it struck me in a way that I wasn't prepared for. Suddenly I was nine, lifting the hatch to his treehouse, and climbing into the only place that would end up making me feel safe.

"Open yours, Mommy." Ellie brought her hands together, excited.

I tore at the wrapping paper and found a glass mason jar. My hands froze, my breath hitched.

Ford came next to me and whispered, "I made a jar of treasure for you like you used to make with grandpa."

Tears filled my eyes immediately as I held the jar full of gold glitter.

"I know you said you used to use sand, but I couldn't find any. I saved this one for you after we made some last night and buried them in the snow. I told everyone it was what you used to do to create magic when you needed it. Last night we needed some, so we made these. I wanted you to have your very own jar on Christmas morning."

My arms were around him as I pulled him into my chest. I continued to cry as Wes explained to Ellie that my tears were happy tears, not sad ones.

Because as I was thinking of how badly I wanted my father to be here with us, he ended up showing up after all.

TWENTY-FOUR
SILAS
TWO WEEKS LATER

It hurt to reach for the lemons, which was going to be a mother fucker to get past, but my doctor said I just needed more recovery time.

Technically I wasn't even supposed to be in the orchard working, but I needed to get back into my routine. While Natty, Rook and Ryle had been taking care of things, there was something therapeutic about being out here, about tending to the fruit and ensuring the trees were healthy.

There was also the nightmare I had last night that was still in my head, still behind my eyelids when I closed my eyes. The orchard on fire, burning so hot that it crawled toward the cottage, and burned my home down too. It was so real, so vivid that it had me reflecting on the Destroyers arriving, and the war they had brought to our doorstep, and then seemingly just disappeared.

Lance explained that Archer Green was the only reason they survived the attack. That them slinking back into the shadows was due to being outnumbered. He'd also told me what he offered in exchange for the Stone Riders leaving the club to get me that doctor. While I knew my best friend would do just about anything for me, the reason I was alive, and Lance had agreed to what he had was all because of Natty.

My wife was a force to be reckoned with when her loved ones were in danger. And for me, I knew she'd move heaven and earth if she had to, just like I would for her. Still, even with them gone, I knew *he* wasn't gone.

"So, you ever going to tell me who he is?" Natty asked, walking up behind me. She had on a pair of jeans, a pair of brown boots and a tattered hoodie that made her look beautiful in a way that shouldn't even be possible.

"Who?"

I turned back toward the orchard and started walking farther into the trees.

"Your brother."

I was turned away from her, so she didn't see my face when she said that. Alec flashed through my mind, his gray eyes so much like my father's. The easy smile he always offered to Natty, the way he was always staring at her. The love he had for her. Then my mind went somewhere dark.

Memories so painful that I had repressed them. An older brother who tortured both Alec and me. Someone made from the exact cut of cloth that Fable had been cut from.

"There's nothing to tell, Caelum."

She had her arms crossed, her green eyes watching me so keenly. Curled pieces of dulled sunshine tucked into a braid, her flawless skin flushed from the cold. I wanted to pull her under my arm, and kiss her.

"Silas, I have your back. Forever. I'll always stand in your corner, on your side of the line, whether it's right or wrong…but for the sake of our sons, I need to know."

That caught my attention, making me turn.

"What do you mean?"

She pulled something from her pocket. "Rook said a man named Max was in the cellar. A man who said he was your brother. He gave this to our son to give to you once you were well enough to process it."

My adrenaline spiked, my heart thrashing around in my chest.

Fingers trembling, I took the note and stared at it.

"Open it," Natty urged, and that made me think she'd already read it.

Unfolding each edge, I slowly opened the letter.

Silas,

I will give you until they're grown to get away from the Stone Riders. I know it was you who killed our father, but I have an old debt with Simon Stone I want to settle with his club. Remove your family from the crosshairs and they'll be spared. I decided to take pity on little Rook, so I will give you until he's graduated and old enough to defend himself if he needs to. You're all more than welcome to fight with me. But I'm coming for them, and if you're in my way, you'll die. Tell your wife, it's time she chooses a side.

-Max

Natty stepped closer.

"Who is he, Silas?"

Natty's whisper had me stepping back, trying to catch my breath.

Rage I hadn't felt since I realized Natty had been hurt by Dirk rushed through me like fire. My wife stepped closer, pressed her lips to my neck, then whispered, "Tell me."

Old memories rushed through my mind, things I never wanted to revisit.

Things I thought I could outrun.

Finally, swallowing the lump in my throat, I answered her.

"He's a monster and they don't show mercy, so this is a lie or a ruse. Either way, we can't trust it."

My wife's face was drawn down in worry. "So what does this mean?"

My shoulder ached, my ribs felt cracked, and this note was only making things worse. But through it, I finally felt some clarity.

"It means we need to make a choice. We either double cross the Stone Riders and hide amongst the Death Raiders, and fight *with* Max."

"Or?" Natty stepped closer, drawing her body flush with mine. It was a tactical move because she didn't like my answer.

I kissed the tip of her nose. "Or we raise our sons as Stone Riders and prepare them for the battle of the century."

"We could always move. Go back to London. I liked London." Natty wrapped her arms around me, squeezing tight.

"Maybe we should...but he's still coming for Killian, and by default his kids, Laura and everyone else tied to the club. That's your family and I know it matters to you if they get hurt. I think it matters to our sons too."

"So we fight?" Natty's face tipped up, and I pressed a kiss to her mouth.

"We fight, and this time, we make sure the Stone Riders are ready for my brother."

The End….
Or at least until next time when the kids grow a bit.

Click here to read Archer's book.

You aren't going to want to miss the connection made in his book, or which world it's going to cross into.

ALSO BY ASHLEY MUÑOZ

Stone Riders Series:

Where We Started

Where We Belong

Where We Promise

Where We Ended

A Rose Ridge Christmas

Mount Macon Series

Resisting the Grump

Tempting the Neighbor

Saving the Single Dad

Standalone

The Rest of Me

Tennessee Truths

Only Once

Rake Forge University Series

Wild Card

King of Hearts

The Joker

Finding Home Series

Glimmer

Fade

Anthology:

Vicious Vet

ACKNOWLEDGMENTS

This was such a fun project but it wouldn't exist without a few friends.

Amanda, your continued encourgment and guidence with this series has been so monumnetal, and so encouraging. This idea to go back to Rose Ridge for a Christmas novella was all you, and I'm so grateful that you told me to do it.

I can't wait for everyone to see what's coming next.

A huge thanks to Echo Grayce for helping us create yet another beautiful cover.

Rebecca Barney, and Tiffany Hernandez, thank you for your editing assistance with this project, and helping me get it where it needed to be.

But more than anything, I want to thank you readers for making The Stone Riders so prevelant, that a Christmas novella was even possible. This series has blown my carrerr into new places I never dreamed of going, and doing things I never imaged it would do. Thank you for loving these characters as much as I do, and for giving me a fresh shot with each book.

Until next time…

ABOUT THE AUTHOR

Ashley is an Amazon Top 50 bestselling romance author who is best known for her small-town, second-chance romances. She resides in the Pacific Northwest, where she lives with her four children and her husband. She loves coffee, reading fantasy, and writing about people who kiss and cuss.

Follow her at www.ashleymunozbooks.com

Join her Newsletter Here

Made in United States
Troutdale, OR
04/06/2025